11-12-15

Dear Hanna,
Hope you enjoy the Story! It was my journey with the Holy Spirit!

Unearthing Christmas

Jesus -
Believe in Him!
Live in Him!
Trust in Him!

Anthea T. Pacaruk

ANTHEA T. PISCARIK

Unearthing Christmas

TATE PUBLISHING
AND ENTERPRISES, LLC

Published by Tate Publishing & Enterprises, LLC
127 E. Trade Center Terrace | Mustang, Oklahoma 73064 USA
1.888.361.9473 | www.tatepublishing.com

Tate Publishing is committed to excellence in the publishing industry. The company reflects the philosophy established by the founders, based on Psalm 68:11,
"The Lord gave the word and great was the company of those who published it."

Cover design by Roland Caballero
Interior design by Gram Telen

Published in the United States of America

ISBN: 978-1-68142-617-4
Fiction / Religious
15.08.28

To all children, for their protection,
purity, and spiritual growth

* * *

Special thanks to Mike for comments and guidance.

Contents

Capturing 1955

In the first week of 1955, John Christmas, his wife, and two of their three children lived in the confines of a bomb shelter outside of Houston, Texas. For three days, they went about the semblance of normal life and its routines. Sanctioned by the US Government, the project was an attempt to assuage national and ultimately worldwide fears of a nuclear attack.

Life magazine's issue of July 11, 1955, featured a side story with photos of the pioneering Christmas family. Starlet Susan Strasburg, daughter of the famed acting coach Lee Strasburg, graced the cover of the cultural icon publication with her fresh-faced beauty so prized in the years before "never too thin or too tan" became the benchmarks of sex appeal. She teases her mouth with a juicy chunk of watermelon while surrounded by enough sliced-up quarters of the red ripe fruit to feed a small village. Yet haunting the image further are the watchful eyes of young boys looking hungrier rather than lust-filled as the sensuous actress nibbles away in oblivion.

The juxtaposition of hard news and pop culture had reached zenith proportions with ubiquitous monthly publications, and *Life* magazine was one of the more prominently displayed on newsstands. Disparaging images of burgeoning celebrities as Miss Strasburg sharing the cover with large-type words "New Red Diplomacy in Action" gave cold, or, actually, cold war comfort for readers all too aware of the underlying threat of extinction. So in all of the dichotomy of dreamlike images and harsh words, a family of five with a name reminding readers of the most joyous of seasons should seem like the appropriate, if not perfect, choice for a rather joyless project taking to task and testing out the realities of the unthinkable—surviving a nuclear war.

Truth is always stranger than fiction, and the truth is that there's something eerie about the notion of a bomb shelter. It's a cellar with a dire purpose, a gloomy, dank, poorly lit tomb-like space giving inhabitants hope that life will continue, if only the time entombed is waited out. Did anyone really think they would use these catacombs for the living? Sure, plenty of newly planted suburbanites were building them, but who really thought they'd spend more than an hour or two in these hidden quarters to simply stock shelves with canned goods and dry foods? True, Londoners survived Hitler's blitzkrieg by descending deep into their subway system or "tube" to escape the bombings from the locust-like warplanes. There's a safe feeling underground, well, unless of course you're in an ornate box with a few dates etched in stone above.

With the nightmarish mushroom clouds imprinted into a global psyche, a subcutaneous life seemed like a workable long shot for survival. The unnaturalness of split atoms and humans turned into mere shadows on paved walkways had been a decade old by 1955, but backyard bomb shelters neared the 1970s. The Christmas family—bored, hot, and endlessly distracted by their restricted environment—were the unsung heroes who proved to the US Defense Department that they could emerge healthy, whole, and reasonably cheerful after a three-day stint. So we go back to a year filled with momentous occasions, at least in the camera's eye. The Christmas family commenced the year, keeping it real in an unreal life capsule. A sleeper hit movie *Marty* won best picture with an anti-leading man, Ernest Borgnine, making a hero out of a lonely Bronx butcher with little to offer a sought-after soul mate other than his big heart. Marilyn Monroe, in her glorious heyday, let the hot air out of comedies by allowing the even hotter air in, or rather under, her chiffon halter dress with a sexpot scene in *The Seven Year Itch*, rivaling any watermelon fest sporting the cover of *Life* magazine. Later that same year, a new reality emerged as Rosa Parks defended her justified right to sit in the front of a

Montgomery, Alabama, bus after a long day at work. Her refusal to change her seat and move to the back of the bus resulted in her arrest and ignited the Civil Rights Movement on December 1. We enter this year, 1955, to sink deep into the ground and unearth a joy that happens only when we look at life through the eyes and in the heart of a child born long ago.

> *St. Andrew's Christmas Prayer.* Hail and blessed be the hour and moment in which the Son of God was born of the most pure Virgin Mary, at midnight, in Bethlehem, in piercing cold. In that hour, vouchsafe, O my God, to hear my prayer and grant my desires, through the merits of Our Saviour Jesus Christ, and of His Blessed Mother. Amen.

1

Ho-Ho, Silver! 1955

Miriam Hopkins fitted the last silvery branch into the aluminum pole. Admiring her work, she stood back while twirling a small pearly button on her cream-colored blouse, a nervous habit that occupied her fingers while her mind raced ahead to the next household chore. Many times, she twisted buttons until the threads gave way and the kitchen sewing kit emerged to prevent yet another interminable button hunt. If a button hunt proved unsuccessful, the wardrobe piece made its way into a special hamper of clothes awaiting buttons, just the right one that would surface in a fabric store or the Lone Star Five & Dime. The hamper housed one green blouse with a ruffle bib, one pink ladies' oxford shirt, and one white dress glove missing a side decorative button. Lorraine, her fourteen-year-old daughter, gazed with disbelief at the tinsel-like branches. She wrinkled her freckled nose in disapproval and adjusted her yellow cloth headband that separated a fringe of bangs from a mass of strawberry blonde hair. Christmas without sweet-smelling pine needles was nothing short of betrayal. She closed her eyes and gave her best grimace.

Tom Hopkins, her bemused father, glanced above the rim of his bifocals. Typically, he dodged any direct requests for taking sides on such matters. Nothing pleased him more than keeping a safe distance from the sparks of angry looks and slamming doors that plagued the Hopkins' household in the last year. Lorraine, affectionately referred to as Lori, tortured her mother with bouts of silence, arm-folding stints, and a general heel-digging attitude of resistance to her mother's demands. He watched his lovely wife work on the button near the base of her throat. *Such an uneasy gesture*, he thought. Why had he not marked it during those days when she lit up the football field as head cheerleader? Probably because he spent most of those early courting days visualizing attempts to unfasten the beastly little plastic, metal, or cloth-covered barriers himself!

Only recently, she made him uneasy with what he considered the most annoying habit imaginable. If only she would simply bite her nails, wring her hands, or smoke a cigarette. No, he knew he was sentenced to a married lifetime of watching his wife's hands clutch her bosom or neck to ease the fears of not getting enough accomplished in a day's time.

"Too space age for me, Mir," said Tom with no elaboration.

Miriam waved a hand of dismissal and patted her auburn chignon. "Nonsense, it's all the rage."

Lori knew she was losing ground by the minute. She fingered a glittery soft branch and said in a whimper, "It's not even green. I hate it."

"You'll get used it, Lori," replied Miriam with a click of her camel-colored pumps. "Now let's decide on a good spot."

"How about the closet?" quipped Lori, watching her mother with mild contempt and slight amusement. She had secreted away a few of those stray buttons orphaned from shirts, coats, gloves, and a skirt or two. Someday, she told herself, she'd confess her wickedness and hand over the collection jar.

Lori's stony look went unnoticed. Miriam surveyed her domicile with one sweeping head turn. A faithful disciple of etiquette expert, Amy Vanderbilt, she prided herself on adopting the very best advice on gracious living. The Hopkins' ranch house, a forerunner of contemporary style, displayed the latest fads: a kidney-shaped coffee table and the butterfly chair. Brown, gold, and orange dominated the color scheme, giving a perpetual autumn feel to the common spaces. Feeling her daughter's stubborn resistance, she quietly said, "Okay then, I'll decide." With quick steps, Miriam made her way through the spacious, modern ranch house into a sleek, teakwood furnished dining area. She took special pride in a room sporting the expensive wood so accommodating to her nontraditional tastes. Recently, she became fond of African artwork and purchased a few masks hung threateningly on the wall opposite a sleek china closet displaying burnt orange ceramic dishes. The charred wooden faces were anything but friendly and peered down at the family like unwanted dinner guests.

"Right here," beamed Miriam, raising her hands as if she just found a buried treasure or the Holy Grail. She extended her hands like a game show model enticing the audience to choose a door hiding a new automobile or kitchen appliance.

Lori's shoulders pitched forward a little with the weight of her disappointment. "A window? What happened to the living room near the fireplace?"

"Fire hazard," chimed in her father.

"We live in Texas for cryin' out loud. We don't even use the fireplace," whined Lori. Even she hated the pitch of her shrill retort and childlike stubbornness. She much rather be inured to her mother's perplexing notion of family life and knack for changing tradition without consulting anyone. *No, those buttons wouldn't be surfacing anytime soon*, she thought with only a shred of smug satisfaction.

At fourteen, well beyond the age of reason, she was occasionally bothered by the unseemly secrets she kept from her mother. Like the time she took money out of her purse to buy a Saturday matinee movie ticket and root beer float at the Lone Star Five & Dime. Joy, her best friend, would plead with her to come clean on these hateful actions, but she never got beyond recounting them to Father Dominic Lavelle behind the privacy of a confessional box at the Church of the Holy Child. Once, after promising her confessor that she would fess up to the misdeed, she complied in a very roundabout manner by strategically leaving confiscated buttons in places her mother would be sure to happen upon. Miriam, the compulsive cleaner, never questioned how these buttons disappeared and reappeared. An irresolute, not totally repentant Lori would give a quick shrug. "I guess St. Anthony heard my prayer." Her reoccurring worry was that someday she would meet St. Anthony face to face and have to account for attributing his intercession without one utterance of a prayer. Miriam knew she won the battle. Every battle. There was no bargaining, and the most she could offer was a shallow response to her daughter's hapless pleas. "We'll hang stockings on the mantle and put our tree in here," beamed Miriam.

Lori pounced at this one. "I thought it was a fire hazard. The stockings would go up in flames, right, Dad? That is, of course, if we actually used the fireplace."

"I think we'll be okay with the stockings," replied Miriam. "They are flame retardant, dear."

With no fighting ground left, Lori succumbed to the loss of a cherished tradition and gave a final, desperate critique of the silver tree. She cupped her chin as if studying a work of art. "It looks like a stack of TV dinner trays."

Miriam yanked at the pearl button at her neck. "It's staying and that's final."

"Enough, young lady. If your mother wants an aluminum tree, well…" Now he'd done it—broken his own rule and jumped off the fence to take a side on the matter. He would much rather rally behind Lori because he sensed her sadness. Tom had seven siblings and knew the joyful, rambunctious noise of family life on a large scale. Texas was new territory for him, and he never dreamed he'd still be living outside of Lubbock in environs so widespread it resembled a prairie outpost.

Born and bred in Boston, Tom met and fell in love with his high school sweetheart. Although he had a few dalliances in college, Mir stole his heart from the first shake of her gleaming auburn hair. Lori, a paler version of her mother, with softer features and freckles, had none of her mother's nervous habits, which he thanked God for daily. But he worried that neuroses would manifest itself somehow, and the tree skirmish was a potential trigger.

Lori conceded defeat, "Well, don't expect me to decorate it."

Her mother softened. "I already bought the ornaments," said Miriam, adjusting a branch. "They are all the same color. Green. I think it will be a lovely accent."

"See that, Pumpkin? We'll have some green."

Lori wondered if her dad was as noncommittal at his job at the manufacturing plant that made plastic resin pellets. She wasn't quite sure what they were or what he did, but his background in chemical engineering led him on a career path winding his way down to the Lone Star state. Tom Hopkins didn't converse much about his work-a-day world, but he did mention the words *defense weapons* to Mir on a few occasions with the effect of her ruining another cardigan sweater with her infuriating habit. Tom had already bought her two new jackets for Christmas—one with a zipper and the other with no fastening devices.

"No lights?" whined Lori, entering the verbal boxing match for one last round.

"It doesn't need any lights or tinsel. Isn't that great?" replied her resolute mom with arms folded and the hint of a smile. "We're doing modern and minimal this year."

Lori heaved a sigh, bordering on despair. "Call me for dinner," she hollered back while heading toward her bedroom.

"Gran's coming over," said Mir in her typically incongruent manner of changing topics.

"And what if she hates it too?" shrieked the disgruntled teenager.

"She helped me pick it out," yelled Miriam.

"I'm doomed," muttered Lori, quietly closing her door.

She passed by her bureau stand and looked hard into the mirror. As a young child, she would spend what seemed like hours staring at her freckles and attempted to count them on one or two occasions. Her mother told her they were kisses from the sun, but Lori prayed nightly that they would disappear by daybreak. She even bought a jar of vanishing cream that promised to magically erase the little brown dots that bridged her nose. A whole jar later, she sported nothing more than a rash that stubbornly persisted an entire month sending her mother into hysterics while dragging her to a dermatologist for remedying what she thought to be an acute case of acne.

A few weeks ago, Gran Mitchell held Lori in a tight hug and whispered, "You need to stop staring at the freckles and start noticing the spaces in between." Her words gave Lori a new perspective of her spotted nose. The clear spaces in between seemed to be growing as her adult years approached. *Maybe, just maybe, my face will grow out of these freckles*, she thought fancifully.

With a huge sigh, Lori dived into a bed full of teddy bears and soft hand-sewn dolls with yarn hair and button-like eyes. She traced an eye on Raggedy Ann, her favorite bed mate. With a deep chuckle, she pictured her mother as a little girl with rag dolls woefully blinded due to missing button eyes.

Christmas would never be the same without the beautiful woodsy scents, wondrous lights, and handmade ornaments attaching memories to each prickly needle branch. And what about pinecones and the soft drizzle of tinsel dripping sparkle? Instead, she'd have an entire tree of tinsel, just one big tinsel town! Rolling over, she picked up Raggedy Ann, tossed her up to the ceiling, and caught her in an absent-minded embrace.

2

Sticks and Stones, 2015

Peggy Mitchell warded off the chilly twilight air by drawing up the frayed collar of her denim jacket.

"There's nothing here," she said, staring at the bare patch of soil. Fingernails bit to the quick scratched repeatedly at the unyielding ground. Fran Dalton crouched down, peering at the clumps of grass bordering the ground marked by a large curved stick. A shock of coal black hair spilled over hazel green eyes. He bent lower.

"This is it. I know from the marker." He rubbed his square, stubbly chin, while clutching a shoebox of portable fuel cell batteries pilfered from the Cutting Edge computer store's warehouse two hours earlier. Priced at $199 retail, the ten batteries would sell for $100 a pop to techies with a blind eye toward hot merchandise.

"We had two grand in that hole, you nimrod," said Larry Lorenzo, puffing on an e-cigarette while pacing and chewing three sticks of spearmint gum.

"Well, you're a big help," shot back Peggy, springing up. She brushed dirt and gravel off her pants and examined a deep tear below her right knee. "Why didn't you tell me we'd be climbing a six-foot fence, anyway? I could have torn off my knee cap!"

"I didn't know they had junkyard dogs," said Fran, rubbing the nape of his neck.

"It's a junkyard, dude, what else would they have? The point is you screwed up. Our money is gone. It's not here and we're losing time," said Larry, pointing his pseudo cigarette at his partner in crime.

At fourteen years of age, all three of the co-conspirators formed a lawless band and practiced regular bouts of shoplifting techno gadgets and reselling the purloined goods. For two years, the profits mounted, keeping them loyal to their woebegone ways and separating them further from the status quo of teenage life. Peggy, like a survivor of anorexia, was reed thin yet strong and energetic enough to run a twenty-mile marathon. Her family had only been in Texas for five years, long enough for Peggy to see her way into a bleak, disenchanted path of teenage drinking, occasional drug use, and low grades. She never blamed the family move for her bad choices, thinking she would have probably been drawn to a similar life in their hometown of Bloomingdale, Indiana, populated with white people resolute on keeping life uncomplicated or hell-bent on making tracks to larger, urban locales.

* * *

The Mitchell family numbered twelve, including Mom and Dad, a preposterous number for living in a double-wide mobile home back in Indiana. Somehow, Peggy's mom made their living quarters practically palatial and a marvel of cozy comfort. With four bedrooms, a large family room, dining room, living room, and kitchen, the Mitchells lived wall to wall. The family room served as a bedroom to the two older boys, Mark and Matthew Mitchell. After Mark and Matthew, came Matilda. The poor child, how she hated her name. Maria and Monica were twins, one tall with blonde curls; the other, short with glossy hair like a midnight waterfall. Soon after their birth, Michael descended on them like the archangel himself, fiery from infancy and truly destined for some form of greatness.

Exactly two years to the day of his birth, Margaret arrived, a sad, colicky infant. She was easily spotted within the brood for never curling her lips into a smile and bearing her pebble-like teeth. She gazed at any photographer in an attempt to figure out why the lens was fixed on her countenance. As if one set of twins wasn't enough for beleaguered Mary Mitchell, yet another set was born less than two years after Margaret. Martin and Martha, the dreamiest, most adorable little bundles slipped into the Mitchell family scene as if they arrived from the beak of a stork. The children marveled at these two perfect children that were the happiness and delight of everyone. They cooed, laughed, and rarely cried, and Mary Mitchell thanked God every day for such a blessing. Two sets of twins brought the number to nine. Peggy surmised there should be only seven siblings even though both sets of twins were fraternal. Of course, the neighbors considered Mary Mitchell more than daft for counting nine children as a blessing! Mr. Hummel, the seventy-year-old bachelor in the two-bedroom trailer next door, would shake his head and mutter, "Yup, that's a baseball team you got there." He repeated the sentiment anytime he saw the Mitchell family together for a Sunday outing. By first grade, Margaret chose the name Peggy to escape the obsessive alliteration her mother manifested through her children.

Well, as Mary Mitchell—one to offer prayers of thanksgiving at least three times a day—wasn't satisfied enough with her blessings, along came the tenth and final Mitchell. Miriam was named after a beloved Aunt from Boston that Peggy only heard reference to once in a blue moon. Of course, some meaning must have been attached to the name since Mary, with her love affair with the letter *M*, had more than enough names to choose from and far from exhausting a potential list. The girls pleaded for Mom to name the new arrival Madeline after the series of cherished books bearing the title. It only seemed fair that she would give in to some family opinion on the matter, especially a name chosen from her numerous offspring since Jack Mitchell disappeared for nearly three weeks at a time in between his coast-to-coast truck routes. He managed to be home for one week per month with enough money for a frugal wife to manage raising now ten children while he spent the balance of time on drinking himself into oblivion. A sober long-distance driver and a drunk father led wife and children wishing his weekly visits over about a day or two, after he kicked his shoes off and fell into a beer-induced slumber. He kept the entire family awake with the deepest most disturbing snoring sessions to ever assault a pair of ears.

Mary Mitchell would repeatedly cross herself and thank God that Jack wasn't a mean drunk and prayed fervently for his soul and a diminishing of his libido that kept her fertile body bearing children. Her only consolation was that he appeared to be faithful, even with the endless temptation of long, lonely stretches of highway time, motel life, and a cadre of road buddies that thought nothing of their private allowance for patronizing prostitutes. Life in the outskirts of Lubbock, Texas was similar to Bloomington only in Mary Mitchell's recreating a cozy home thanks to her indefatigable nature of wearing rose-colored glasses and praying every day for the intercession of St. Monica, patroness of all mothers. She had a framed picture of the long-suffering saint, an iconographic image with flat, grim features and a stern glance hanging in the family room wall next to a split image of the Immaculate Heart of Mary and the Sacred Heart of Jesus both exposing their inflamed, pierced hearts. Mary Mitchell was all smiles and dimples and wavy red hair, like a displaced Celtic fairy. Peggy adored her mom.

Someday, she thought, *I will turn the corner and come clean.* But it wouldn't be today, tomorrow, or even next week.

* * *

Peggy, Fran, and Larry stood motionless above the table of barren ground. Fran's inexhaustible attempt to keep the black curtain of hair out of his eyes only subjected him to a constant jerk of his head and any observer to slight dizziness. The nervous tick exasperated Larry, already nearing the point of inner rage.

"Well, I had to throw the suckers over the fence," mumbled Fran. "I hope nothin' broke."

"Nah, the only thing that's gonna break is your nose when it meets my fist," threatened Larry, spitting out the tasteless gum.

"Yeah, and then it will look like yours, going three directions at once," rejoined Fran with a self-conscious smirk. Peggy grew tired of their barking and growling at each other like two frightened dogs baring teeth with no intention of breaking skin. Fran continued, "Okay, let's regroup and get this stuff buried. We know where we are. The stick is here, right? We're all witnesses now, right?"

With fierce determination, Peggy cleared loose rocks, stones, or pieces of gravel while Fran and Larry watched. "Are you two going to help me dig?" Her impatience mounted while observing the late autumn sky turn a blended shade of crimson and pink announcing an imminent sunset. "I don't have a flashlight, so we need to get this done," Peggy continued moving rocks and stones around to mark the spot.

"Why do we have to bury this stuff, anyway?" griped Fran, combing through his hair.

"Because it's way too hot," replied Peggy in frustration.

She observed her companions with a special tenderness she would normally reserve to a stray animal or injured bird. She understood pain in a way no one else could, even if self-inflicted. When Fran was nine years old, she spied him cheating on a test, his hands covered with ink, actually written words that held the answer key. Once completed, he turned his paper in, excused himself, went to the bathroom, and returned with all evidence scrubbed away. Peggy's mom frequently said her little renegade never missed a trick. Larry was another story. He had money and didn't want for anything, other than the affections of a mom and dad who unwittingly dismissed him. The void in family life was filled with uncharitable acts of stealing not only merchandise from local dollar or chain department stores but school lunches and money for cafeteria purchases. If there was a vote on the most disliked individual in all of high school freshman year, Larry would win with a landslide. Peggy saw the bully's flip side. The power and domination, so evidenced by anyone in Larry's company, was only the mask or protective covering for a lonely child that grew angrier with each year of emotional solitude. His parents, owners of a butcher shop, rarely spent time with their only child who, like a Rocky Balboa wannabe, would pound sides of beef with his fists in the freezer locker. If only Mr. and Mrs. Lorenzo knew the violent blows and hot tears were meant for them. *Someday*, thought Peggy, *a beautiful, gentle, kind, and loving core would emerge from the rage*. She wanted to be there when the metamorphosis took place. Meanwhile, he smoked his smokeless cigarettes, an attempt to quit tobacco, and engaged in petty crimes to feed his fury.

"We got nothing to dig with here," snapped Larry with a flick of imaginary ashes.

"Yeah, poor planning, huh?" added Fran, now clutching the nape of his neck. Peggy dreaded another bully versus bullied dance between the two of them. She quickly interjected.

"Our hands," she said with a determined stare.

"Too hard," grumbled Larry, kicking at the dirt with stabs of his heel. His negative, cheerless demeanor was an added cross to bear for his companions.

"No, it isn't," countered Peggy with grim determination to lead the threesome out of their present dilemma. She was the reluctant leader of their escapades, not because she enjoyed her delinquency, but simply because she felt a maternal quality in every relationship. Her matriarchal family experience had left an indelible mark in her psyche. She knew her mother was the centering force in the quietly chaotic existence of their Texas home.

Why they moved to Texas was still a mystery to her. With Dad gone most of the time, Indiana seemed like as good a place as any to build a life. Not good enough for the man of the house, or so he thought he was when he returned to disrupt an orderly, peaceful existence for Mark, Matthew, Matilda, Maria and Monica, Michael, Margaret (a.k.a. Peggy), Martin and Martha, and Miriam the baby. He would look at his children as if he wondered where they came from, scratching and shaking his head. Peggy wondered how many of his children he'd actually witnessed being born, but she never asked. She liked keeping him at an emotional distance. Her saintly mother never uttered a word against him, especially since he always paid the bills.

Peggy preferred Bloomingdale, a small town in the middle of nowhere. She didn't like living so close to Lubbock, on the edge of a nondescript city in the middle of nowhere. Clearing her mind, she focused on the ground below her feet and started pulling up prairie grass, dirt, and loose rocks. Fran and Larry stood by like watchmen ready to go off duty. She picked up a large stick and clawed at the dirt with ferocity. After a few minutes of digging, she glanced up at her accomplices.

"Well, are you going to help out here or what?" she grumbled, irritated at their insouciance.

"It's getting late," said Fran, feeling a guilty pang at a deepening desire to bolt.

"That's why we need to finish up," whined Peggy. "We've got to get rid of this stuff now. None of us can take it home." Without faltering, she dug a few inches more until the stick felt the tug of something akin to a fishing line. "What's this?" Peggy pulled at the line.

"It's probably a land mine or something," joked Larry, puffing away.

Peggy leaned in to get a closer look. She felt around, brushing away any excess dirt from the uncovered article. Sitting atop the earthen table was a string of velvety, red poinsettias. She continued to gently tug, exposing more of the unusual find in the middle of an abandoned field.

"Someone's holiday trash. Maybe this was a dumping site," remarked Larry.

"Weird, huh? Let's keep digging." With persistent enthusiasm, Peggy pulled on the string of red and green garland. No one in the Mitchell clan liked Christmas more than Peggy, and the symbol of her favorite time of year gave her a curious hope to find some additional items.

"Why? We're good," chimed in Fran. "Let's just throw the stuff in there and cover it up." Fran favored being home to spending time dallying on his misadventures. He so much appreciated his sanctuary of a room, alone and without the complications of dealing with other people, anyone actually.

The youngest of three, his other siblings were highly accomplished. Fred, a recent college graduate, was now pursuing a master's degree in biomedical research. As the oldest, he never liked Fran and barely recognized his mortal existence. With an eight-year age difference, they lived in separate worlds, and he always considered his younger brother a shiftless usurper of the world's resources. He knew that Fran cheated on tests, noticing the ink marks on his hands while driving him to school on a rainy Monday four years ago. Realizing full well his little brother's intentions, he urged him to study hard and be disciplined in schoolwork. The preaching fell upon deaf and disinterested ears. No one cared less about school than Fran, or so even he observed about himself. Homework was optional, typically unfinished and stashed under his bed. Both of his siblings, Fred and Nora, were overachievers receiving endless praise from parents who took bragging rights to an extreme. Fran was the self-appointed underachiever. He was sure someday he would find a passion for some field of interest, possibly zoology, forestry, maybe even cetology being inclined to prefer the company of God's amphibious creatures. His aquarium, meticulously cared for, held all of his submerged family bearing names and fictitious lives behind their glass box. His personal ennui would vanish when in the company of his finned friends. Somehow, someday, he believed he would emerge a new and sanctified individual, shedding his teenage angst like the skin of a garden snake he stumbled upon a year ago. He held on to this faint image of a new creation in the midst of his lying, cheating, and indolence.

"It's a long piece of garland," remarked Peggy. Her interest in the forlorn decoration deepened.

"I really think we're done here," repeated Fran, growing even more impatient than his fidgety friend, Larry.

He and Larry were opposite ends of the spectrum, physically and in every mannerism. Fran—tall, lanky, and soft-spoken—appeared like some kind of incarnation of Jughead from the old

Archie comics with his blue-black hair and slow reaction time. Behind the head jerking, hands in pocket, quiet demeanor was a professor-like brilliance and mental agility to be a greater academic achiever than Fred and Nora, who he affectionately referred to as Dread and Snora, one being just awful and the other being awfully boring. Larry was a raging bull of a person, compact, muscular, and downright mean most of the time. His peers feared him because of his unpredictable outbursts whether punching a vending machine on the blink, or endless name-calling to anyone crossing his path. He was the butcher's brute of a son, and only Peggy and Fran would spend time in his company. They both understood the prison he created with his rawness in social mores and considered him simply a diamond in the rough awaiting the instruments to cut through the rock for the shiny stone to emerge.

"We really can't dig no more." Larry grew tired of the latest exploit. The rush of getting away with misdeeds was usually followed by a vague sense of indifference.

Fran checked his watch. "Yeah, we're done, Peggy."

"Okay, okay. But I'm coming back here tomorrow with a shovel." Peggy's dogged determination was getting the best of her. She didn't understand why a vintage reminder of Christmas would stir her to an exhaustive excavation with no apparent reward.

Fran, already checked out, eyed his watch barely visible with a darkening sky. "Why?"

"I'm in. Maybe our cash is still here. I'll come back and help." Larry was constantly seeking out a reason to be close to Peggy. Sometimes, he imagined her as a sister and confidante, and other times, as a soul mate.

Everyone liked Peggy. She was oftentimes as nonthreatening and approachable as a lamb in a petting zoo. The infrequent pitchy rages ignited by a thoughtless slur were easily forgiven, if not forgotten, by the offender. Larry was well aware of being a ferocious lion who only the bravest tamer would ever approach. Fran was simply an intelligent gorilla, peeling away at a banana and minding his own business.

"Alright, alright, I'm in." Fran scratched his head and pulled hard on his bangs. His business sense was kicking in to overdrive. "But we need to get the merchandise out of here by Monday."

"Three days from now. We're good." Larry tucked away his placebo in a shirt pocket and zipped up his jacket. "Hey, I think this might work."

"You mean selling this stuff? There's always a market for hot stuff." Fran's agitation grew as he thought about his angel fish, Leticia, looking pale and unreceptive to flake food or dried blood worms for nearly two weeks. She was the oldest fish in the tank, and he knew she wouldn't survive much longer.

"No, bozo brain. The smoking. I've been off the cancer sticks for two weeks now."

Larry doesn't need a flame to ignite his temper, thought Fran.

Peggy covered up her find with loose dirt and set the stick in place like a grave marker. Maybe if the poinsettia garland was fully intact, she could use it for the family Christmas tree. She would handle it carefully and sponge off decades of grime with a gentle detergent. The notion of such a simple act of cleansing gave her mild comfort and elicited a genuine smile from normally pursed lips.

3

Ink Spots

Lori fidgeted in her desk and fingered the deep round hole that once held an ink bottle. How strange to imagine students or any writer dipping endlessly into an inkwell to write blotchy letters on parchment paper. Her Bic ballpoint pen was a sleek, efficient instrument that kept the scribe in her scrawling every word uttered by a droning history or sociology teacher. She felt the smooth, slender cylinder in her hand and was reminded of the aluminum Christmas tree now adorning the large-framed dining room window. It stood starker than ever with midday sunlight shining through and baring its artificiality in an almost punishing way. An illumined, flickering image on the white screen flooded the shaded classroom. A large mushroom cloud filled the wall with the stark reality of nuclear war. Lori had seen this image a dozen times throughout her school years. For five years, she witnessed—only from footage—the large unnatural cloud consuming everything in its path. Many times, she wondered what actually happened to the flora and fauna immediately in its path. She heard stories of people disintegrating within a split second. Jake Dugan switched off the film projector and turned on the classroom lights. Lori didn't mind Mr. Dugan's somberness because he had dreamy, blue eyes like a twilight sky. She'd never seen eyes so dark and lambent all at once. His years of high school and college football left him with a set of wide, muscular shoulders and arms that framed his angular body and diminished the nascent stages of a paunch.

She studied the sketch she'd drawn in her notebook. So many times, she'd seen some version of a woman stocking shelves in a fallout shelter that she could copy the image blindfold. Fallout shelters, or more frequently referred to as bomb shelters, were common and being built in backyards throughout Texas and the entire country.

"Okay, class, that's all we have time for today." Mr. Dugan wore a tired expression on his face. Peggy wondered why he wasn't married and thought him doomed for bachelorhood. Her math teacher, Miss O'Donnell, a petite blonde, with prominent cheekbones, usually perked up whenever in his company, but he barely noticed her as his partner chaperone at the school dances.

* * *

Lori pushed along a tray in the cafeteria line, adding a hot dog and glass of lemonade. The din of high schoolers trading secrets and fresh gossip quieted the discontent in her heart. Christmas was appearing less like anything to celebrate, let alone anticipate, and she wanted to recapture the joy. She noticed her friend and usual lunch partner, Joy Lieberman, approaching her.

Lori chuckled to herself. "Joy, I was just thinking of you."

Joy slid a tray of macaroni and cheese across the table and plopped down next to her longtime schoolmate. She dug her fork into a pile of glossy noodles, holding it up for inspection.

"Mac and cheese again. They're intent on killing our taste buds." Lori always felt balanced out and comforted by her childhood comrade who knew every one of her secrets, including crushes, and, yes, the button thievery.

"Ready for the Christmas dance? I bought a new skirt. It's all the rage," said Joy, slurping a forkful of noodles.

"Lemme guess. It's got a big poodle."

"And chain!" added Joy with her usual aplomb. Lori finished up her doodling efforts—a bomb shelter complete with provisions. Distracted by her drawing, she announced, "Joy, they're not new. Poodle skirts have been around for almost ten years."

"Not around here. Tell me what you're wearing." Joy was reminded of how easily her best friend was drawn into a world excluding everyone else. Yet it was the essence of Lori's aloofness that she respected and admired.

"My dad built one of these," replied Lori, studying her sketch.

Joy saw no way to redirect the conversation. She'd been preparing for weeks for the dance, even heading up a special committee of the Pep Club to have a say in decorations, refreshments, and music.

"Okay, I give up. Built what?" Leaning across the table, she glanced over her friend's art work. "A bomb shelter?"

"Like in the movie we just saw for the third time?" replied Lori.

Joy stabbed at the last few forkfuls of her macaroni and cheese with renewed interest, while Lori pushed aside her untouched grub. "So what's your point?" Joy fingered one of her ash blonde corkscrew curls that framed her countenance with its apple cheeks and tiny mouth enlarged with carefully applied ruby red lipstick.

"I dunno. Never gave it much thought." Lori sipped at the lemonade and bit into the cold hot dog before tossing it back on the plate.

"So tell me what you're wearing to the dance. Aren't you excited? I can't wait. We have a live act this year. Some guy from Memphis. I forget his name." Lori gave a blank stare. Joy waved a hand in front of her. "Are you even listening? We have a live act. The same new bebop singer that was here back in October at the Fair Park Coliseum."

Lori refocused. "Yeah, I heard, and you don't even remember his name. I'll figure something out to wear, if I go." One final gulp of lemonade and she pushed aside the littered tray. "So do you believe that stuff about bombs and shelters?"

"Who cares? It'll never happen again." Joy rummaged through her deep skirt pockets. "Wait a minute, I have it written down somewhere from the Pep Club meeting. Here it is." Producing a creased sheet of loose leaf paper, she carefully unfolded it like a treasure map. "Oh yeah, that's it. Elvis. Elvis Presley."

"I heard of him. Bet he's no Buddy Holly. Now he's going places!" Lori picked up her tray and abruptly ended their lunch session. "Hey, Joy, I just remembered I have to talk with Miss Jordan before home ec. Something about a special project I'm working on. I'll catch you later." She paused and smiled back at her dearest friend and pseudo sister. "Yeah, I'll probably go to the dance. I mean, how bad can this guy be, right?"

On her way home from school, Lori hugged her textbooks close to her powder blue corduroy jacket. Christmas was merely two weeks away and feeling like a million light years beyond her emotional grasp. A car horn honked as she strolled along the paved sidewalk. She glanced up long enough to see Christine Milford hanging out the window of her father's car and waving furiously. Slung and tied to the back of their red and white Bel Air convertible was a pine tree with soft green needles awaiting the soft glow of lights and neatly wrapped gifts tucked under its lowest branches.

At home, Lori tossed her books onto her white eyelet canopied bed and went to work with single-minded determination. With the house to herself, she sighed a deep sense of satisfaction. Her mission: steeping herself in Christmas and creating the familiar world of incandescent lights, shiny ornaments, and irrepressible joy. Breezing through each room, she headed toward a narrow hallway closet and poked a mop handle at the crawl space board. Positioning a ladder, she gingerly ascended to awaiting ornament boxes and various containers filled with seasonal memories. Feeling around the crowded space, Lori came upon an album with a film of dust coating its cover. Intrigued, she descended the ladder to carefully examine her new find.

"Ink Spots? Wow, they're still popular!" She scanned the date printed in the corner: 1939, two years before she was born. Loaded down with boxes of treasured ornaments and the Ink Spots record, Lori headed back to her sanctuary. She passed by the bare aluminum tree with its feeble attempt to fill a picture window. Even if stylish, it simply wasn't showcase worthy. Lori wasn't sure why she hated the innocuous piece of metal, a shape-shifter that barely resembled life-giving trees with their fruits, seeds, nesting places, soft leaves, or sharp needles. With a shrug of her shoulders, she marched off to her mission of sorting through her collection. Once in her room, she placed the album on her phonograph, and watched it spin the melodious tune of "If I Didn't Care," a song she instantly recognized from her mother humming or singing the lyrics. Even as a child, she wanted the lyrics to be about her and no one else. Lori replayed the song five times. "If I didn't care would it be the same? Would my ev'ry prayer begin and end with just your name? And would I be sure that this is love beyond compare? Would all this be true if I didn't care for you?"

She thought about her mother as a young woman close to her age listening to songs of romantic dreams as the world entered a period of nightmarish global strife. Lori was practically a newborn when Pearl Harbor was attacked and had no memories of fireside chats and updates of battlefront news. Similarly, she only possessed vague impressions of the Korean War, which had little impact on her youth since her mother didn't encourage conversation at the dinner table. Typically, her idle chatter was limited to the latest celebrity updates from her *Photoplay* magazines.

"If I didn't care," crooned Lori along with the words from the worn vinyl disc. Many times, she thought her mother cared less for anything else but drapes and dinnerware, the manifestation of her certain brand of vanity and such a remarkable contrast to her general discomfort for life and odd collection of nervous habits. Lori yearned for the maternal love that would give her feelings of deep peace, loving security, and abiding joy. At this moment, her mother was an impenetrable force dominating their home with some sense of meaningless fashion. Listening to the Ink Spots and their deeply melodic voices, she suddenly felt mawkish for her silly notions of a song so obviously a tribute to lovers, not familial sentiments.

"What does she care about?" whispered Lori aloud. A knock on the front door and a faint yell interrupted Lori's silent remonstration of her mother's peculiar ways. *It's the betrayer*, thought Lori while lifting the vinyl disc off her phonograph.

"Lori, dear, are you home?" Gran Mitchell removed her beige coat of fine wool and matching beret, draping them across a dining room chair. She studied the tinsel-branched tree that Lori resolutely insisted was ruining Christmas.

What did it matter, anyway? she thought, finding it difficult to make an argument either way. As much as she cherished both her daughter and granddaughter, she believed her family role was as peacemaker, or more accurately, fence-sitter.

* * *

A retired nurse, Lottie was educated and refined, having seen the ravages of two world wars on young men sacrificing limbs and lives. Recalling her private tête-à-tête last week with a miserable and pouting Lori, Gran understood disappointment and did her best at consoling with kind words and a warm bearlike hug. Gran, or Charlotte, was better known as Lottie. Her mother was a great admirer and friend of Lottie Moon, the famed Southern Baptist missionary who died Christmas Eve, 1912, on a ship bound for the United States from China. With years of toiling in her beloved mission field behind the Great Wall, Lottie Moon was worn to death and barely fifty pounds at her arrival in a port in Japan where she gave up the ghost. Her namesake, Lottie Mitchell, remembered hearing the tragic news from her mother and wondered why religious fervor would take any mortal to the extremes of punishing the physical body. As a Southern Baptist herself, Lottie never dreamed her own life would take such dramatic twists and turns, leading to the Yankee roots of Boston with its arctic blast winters. She converted to Catholicism after meeting and marrying John Mitchell, a tall, handsome surgeon with skilled hands and a tender heart. Nearly five years after his death, her sense memory enlivened the touch of his strong yet gentle, caressing fingers on her cheek and tracing the nape of her neck. Lottie remembered the day of reckoning when she announced to her Virginia-bred parents that she'd met and fallen in love with the Bostonian man of her dreams.

A year or so earlier, at the seemingly ripe old age of twenty-seven, she had resigned herself to maidenhood and her vocation as a teacher in rural Virginia. A friendly appeal letter from an uprooted classmate, Josie Moore, lured her to a Christmastime visit and tour of an inner-city public school in Boston. By day two, she was ready to pack her bags and leave the tundra-like existence of the peculiar Beantown where Irish and Italians held court and prominence. Toughing out the week, she grew a liking to the plethora of social outings for an unmarried woman nearing thirty. Returning to Virginia, she continued corresponding with Josie and warmed up to the idea of returning for another visit in the spring. As fate dictated, her second visit was the start of her new life. With the country now engaged in a world war, Lottie felt a call to duty and signed up for the Vassar Training Camp in 1918 set up to train college graduates under a three-month intensive program to enter schools of nursing. There, she met a young doctor with piercing blue eyes who towered above the other gents dedicated to the field of medicine. Their lives intertwined as neatly as any fairy tale could weave. As fate would have it, they worked side by side in a field hospital in France, only ten miles away from the frontline where they witnessed shell shock, mortal wounds, and cases of poison gas inhalation. What grew along with their deep caring for each other was an even deeper respect that was forged by realizing a calling to serve others and save lives. It wasn't an arrogant notion, quite the opposite. Humility and service were at the core of their every action. They were too similar for words, like the new Adam and Eve trying to set the course of salvation on right footing.

Whatever passion they had for each other was thrown into their hospital duties, and so many soldiers benefited from their benevolent and grace-filled spirits and inspired dedication to saving lives. When they returned stateside, John nearly lost his beloved Lottie to the Great Influenza epidemic, and he prayed unceasingly for her recovery. So many lives were lost, and he made an unspoken promise to God that if his beloved died, he would leave medicine and commence study for the priesthood, even at his mature age when so many younger men entered the ordained life after youthful years of study and preparation. Miraculously, Lottie rallied and regained full health and attributed rosaries and novenas to her cure. If only her mother and father understood, even the slightest modicum of her deep conversion of heart, maybe they would accept, if not embrace, her newfound faith. She tempered her devotion to the Blessed Mother and Catholicism when in their company but was adamant about marrying John Mitchell.

One year to the day they were married, Miriam was born to adoring parents. She was an irresistible child with dimples, blue eyes, and strawberry blonde curls, a southern belle born in Boston. Within a few years, Lottie was sorely missing her vocation as a nurse. Although the war had ended and life was filled with comforts, good friends, and an adorable child, Lottie was a social being, and meeting the needs of a demanding toddler proved unfulfilling and tedious. Changing diapers was a far cry from changing the blood-soaked dressing on a terrified yet brave soldier barely out of his youth who survived a bullet wound or explosion. Her personal dissatisfaction went unseen by John, a highly skilled surgeon who established himself as a preeminent heart specialist during a period when bypass surgeries were rare, patients practiced upon, and, hopefully, saved on the operating table. Lottie recalled her early years as a first-time mother and lamented her selfish preoccupations. Perhaps Miriam was cognizant of her mother's emotional distance, even as a babe and toddler.

Children are keen, at every age, and Miriam was ultra-observant and overly sensitive to her environment. Fragility marked her mannerisms, and even now, Lottie could see the button twisting as Miriam's remedy for shattered nerves in addition to popping an occasional sleeping pill or prescribed sedative lining her medicine cabinet. Many times, Lottie thought her daughter was one stray button away from losing her mind. All of Lottie's renewed hopes and dreams rested in Lori, a child so pleasant that a mere hint of her smile could light up a curtain-drawn room. Finding her so troubled was doubly troubling, especially knowing she, her loving

Gran, was a contributing agent. Lottie succumbed to her daughter's wishes all too quickly with an endless goal of assuaging the nagging guilt. Admittedly, the aluminum tree was unremarkable in taste and decor and a contradiction to the naturalness of a wooden manger, central to the season. Putting aside her own opinion was the dance she engaged in with Miriam in the last few years. Now she was determined to offer a peace pipe with the freckle-faced delight of her life. Lori crouched cross-legged on her carpet, reading the words printed on the album sleeve.

"Hi, Pumpkin. You okay?" Lottie jumped on the bed and succumbed to a tangle of dolls and plush animals.

A purposely silent Lori studied the album cover. A tossed penny landed in her lap, and she took her cue. "You always give in to her." Lori threw the album cover across the floor, imagining a spray of inky spots dotting her carpet.

"Tell me more." Lottie was the queen of coaxing, and Lori knew the drill.

"You know what's bothering me, so I don't really want to talk about it." Lottie waited out the silence. "Okay, I'll tell you what's bothering me. The pole with tinsel branches. I need it to disappear. It's ruining our Christmas."

"You mean your Christmas?" Lottie learned long ago, with a straight shooter husband, to keep an argument focused.

"Okay, so it's my Christmas, but I have a plan."

Lottie lifted herself from Lori's childhood menagerie of bedmates. "Tell us more."

"You mean tell you more?"

With outstretched arms circling the bed and a widening grin, Lottie rebutted, "No, I mean us." She coddled Peggy's beloved Raggedy Ann. "We're all ears." There it was, the smile that could keep a candle lit in a wind tunnel.

"I'm spending Christmas in Dad's bomb shelter."

4

Bunker Heels

Franny relived every sunrise as a fresh start and every sunset as a return to burning resentment. No day went by without revisiting the abhorrence he felt for family, namely his siblings with their veneer of haughtiness and scorn for the gawky brother who lied and cheated his way through life. Why Franny didn't buy into their disdain was an act of sheer will because inside he understood the remonstrations and constant advice to go clean with his life. Their real concern was that he would tarnish their name, and it needled him constantly any time he gave them a thought in a day's time. His resentment crumbled the foundation of any healing or remorse for his actions. At least five times a day, he wished he were an only child, even if such thoughts were puerile and unfounded. A text message appeared on his phone as he glanced for a time check. "WRU?"

Tapping a quick answer, "AH," Fran suddenly realized he was half an hour late for his sunrise rendezvous with Peggy and Larry.

Guessing as much, Peggy's thumbs got busy. "URUNBLEFBLE."

Fran zipped up the crumpled jeans tossed on his natty dresser the night before. He sprinkled a few fish food flakes in his aquarium, grabbed a jacket, and raced out the door while the living room grandfather clock chimed the half hour of seven thirty. A week ago, he figured out a way to silence the bells that ring out every quarter hour, impelling him to wrap a goose-feathered pillow around his head muffling the incessant bong. His mom, thinking her beloved German clock was running out of time, called in Lubbock's reigning timepiece expert who had it in working condition before a full day of fifteen minutes went by, and the cling-clang, once again, echoed against the walls.

"Where is the loser?" Larry's patience was wearing thin, and he cursed under his breath at the thought of losing precious sleep, his favorite pastime.

Peggy checked her phone. "SRY BRT."

"He'll be right here."

Then it happened, the inevitable tinge of remorse surfaced. It never went away. Waiting for Fran underscored the wrong they were doing. Maybe her life would start over again. Peggy didn't believe in reincarnation, but she sure hoped she'd have different lives in the one she was given.

"Do you ever worry about getting caught, I mean with the stuff?" Peggy studied the quickly rising sun and waited for a response from her explosive cohort. A question begging for some reflection could set him off.

"Sure I do," replied Larry in a subdued tone rarely heard.

Peggy continually guessed he had a soft side. She turned to look at the stocky young man as he jabbed away at the resilient ground, a death grip on the shovel. Only on rare occasions did he utter any words in a hushed voice, and it usually was in response to a stray cat or dog showing some scar of abuse or a tearjerker movie, once again, with a four-legged creature as its hero. Now logic would dictate that most humans respond kindly to animals in distress, but Larry became a sobbing idiot, blinking back and wiping away tears. The only time she ever observed him praying was when he brought a striped feral cat to the SPCA after its tail had been whacked off. He carried the hurt and abandoned creature in his arms like a baby and stayed with Whiskers, a quickly adopted name, until the SPCA vet provided antibiotics and a modicum of comfort to the frightened feline. If Larry ever changed his ways, he could rival St. Francis of Assisi as the patron saint of animals. He had no pets of his own but saved numerous cats, dogs, turtles, birds, both winged and four-legged creatures in his path. She pondered why he had no feelings for the poor carcasses hanging in his parents' butcher shop. Or maybe he did.

They waited, and from a distance, Fran's lanky frame came into view. Larry dug ferociously with no intention of acknowledging his tardy friend. Peggy was amused at how his emotional meter could go from zero to ten—total reluctance to complete absorption with a project. One deeper dig and the shovel met its match: metal against metal.

Fran approached and quickly surveyed the scene. "Wow, it's an underground shelter." The mission was upon them.

Opening up the heavy basement door, Peggy shivered at the thought of agitated snakes, spiders, and slimy creatures. Descending down a half-dozen or more steps, Peggy, Larry, and Fran flashed lights on the oblong cellar with thick cement walls. Christmas decorations abounded on shelves stocked with snow globes, knitted stockings, antique dolls, and volumes of children's fairy tales piled in with fashion magazines. A small green pine tree with bulbous painted lights and hand-blown glass ornaments adorned the middle of the room. Larry approached a musty, dusky corner with a free-standing blackboard leaning against the gray, crushed stone.

"Hey, check this out," he yelled back to Peggy and Fran. Spotting with his flashlight, he read the message written in red and green chalk, "Merry Christmas, 1955." Picking up an eraser, Larry poised it against the milestone marker.

Peggy shot across the room and snatched it away. "No, don't," she said in a reprimanding tone.

Sheepishly, he replied, "I want to write my own message."

Peggy's frustration surfaced. "Are you serious?" Pointing to the potential victim of Larry's mercurial ways, she added, "That message was written sixty years ago."

Fran, the laconic third party, chimed in, "Theoretically."

Peggy sized up her two accomplices. How much longer could she continue the game? The bad girl with her life of petty crime and disillusionment. One day it, whatever it turns out to be, will play out like a poker round leading nowhere until, with total abandon, everyone around the table folding and walking away. A mind and soul scrubbed clean was her silent wish, if not prayer.

"Theoretically?" she repeated in a shrill tone. "It's real. Why do you question everything?" Peggy was armored for the rash of sparse yet rational arguments from the thinker.

"Well, we found it. Couldn't someone else?"

"I doubt it." Peggy, arms folded, eyed Larry as he touched every Christmas artifact in easy reach.

"Yeah, kind of creepy, huh?" Larry moved around the concrete rectangle, scoping out what he might score. "Hey, check this out," he bellowed from another corner of the room. "A record player already loaded up." Lifting the arm, he examined the vintage machinery.

Peggy practically leaped across the room. "Don't touch it. You'll scratch the needle."

"Needle?" Larry leaned closer.

Fran sauntered over for an inspection. Carefully lifting the needle, he blew off a weighty dust ball. "I think it still works." Taking a handkerchief out of his back pocket, he wiped it gently across the grooves of the black disc, while Larry and Peggy watched in silence. Fran had a sensitivity that resonated in every situation. The present one was no exception. He turned the side knob and the glossy black plastic spun slowly as he set the needle back in place. The sultry voice of singer Eartha Kitt, warbling "Santa Baby," echoed throughout the vault. Furthering his investigation, Larry spotted his next curiosity, a television screen framed inside a wooden console.

"Check this out. Wow, I wonder if this TV works." He searched nearby. "Where's the remote?"

"Remote? Hey, doofus, we're in 1955 here, remember?" Peggy leaned over and turned a dial next to the picture screen. The box warmed up to a bright, ghostly image of Ed Sullivan, the variety show host with a deadpan delivery of premiere live acts brought to living room viewers for nearly three decades. Pointing to a curtain offstage, the camera switched over to an ice arena with a gleam-eyed Scandinavian carving her blades across the slick surface. Peggy watched, mesmerized and dazzled.

"What's this?" Larry reached for the channel knob.

"No, leave it alone," snapped Peggy.

"What gives with you and the control freak thing?" Larry backed off, digging fingers into the inner pocket of his jacket.

"Larry, no cigarettes, fake or real. I don't trust what's going on in here. And there's a live tree, if you hadn't noticed." Peggy's commanding voice kept Larry on edge as he paced about like a caged circus lion.

Cross-legged, Fran sat on the floor, taking in the graceful and athletic figure skater. "This show is airing live! December 25, 1955."

5

Untold Truths

Tom Hopkins crunched a spoonful of cornflakes while propping the *Lubbock Avalanche-Journal* against the Kellogg's cereal box. Lori conceded her dad was building a breakfast fort to shun the Hopkins females and protect himself from any interruption to his morning routine.

Lori and Miriam shared a Thomas English muffin smothered in butter and Concord grape jelly, part of their special morning ritual unless they were not on speaking terms. With a silent resolution to recreate Christmas, Lori ate her half muffin with more relish than usual. The aluminum tree, with bits of light reflecting from its fake branches, shone brilliantly in the large picture window from early sunrise to sunset, in opposition to nature's first rays and closing curtain.

Lori crunched on her last buttery nook and cranny. Tom studied the folded newspaper as if conducting a scientific lab experiment. Lori flipped through a recent Christmas catalog while entertaining the visions of proverbial sugarplums dancing in her head. Miriam, matriarch and head mistress of her dining table, jotted down notes on a piece of paper. She routinely created shopping and chore lists to organize the day, at least in her head.

Disrupting the morning silence, Tom spoke from behind his barricade, "Listen to this, Mir."

"What's that, dear?" Miriam welcomed the transition from quiet to a small chat.

"Remember the story about the Houston family named Christmas? They lived in a bomb shelter for three days."

"That's nice," uttered Miriam, instantly disinterested.

Lori made her move, miraculous as it seemed, for the conversation going exactly in the direction she had intended. "I think we should try it," she said enthusiastically.

"Try what?" replied Miriam, returning attention to her list.

"Living in Dad's bomb shelter." Lori smiled smugly with a loosely cupped hand resting on her jawbone.

"Why on earth would we do that?" Miriam barely hid the smirk rising from some deep place within her that periodically left her disturbed.

Why was she always ready to pounce on her only daughter, her only child, who lived and breathed to feel a shower, or even a light sprinkling of affection? How could she know this truth and not respond lovingly? Was it knowledge of the box of lost buttons that kept her secretly disappointed and possibly a little loathing of her precious offspring? Many times, she contemplated exposing the mean-spirited act but believed it better to wait, simply wait for her daughter to come clean. Somehow, she knew Lori would eventually confess to her silent crime in good time. If she really wanted to punish Miriam, she would have simply thrown away the purloined buttons, never to be resurrected, never to be acknowledged, and, possibly, tragically, resulting in an even greater loss—the opportunity for reparation, recompense, and, ultimately, forgiveness. She awaited a confession and kept knowledge of the misdeed to herself.

Mr. Hopkins opened up his breakfast fort, moving away the cereal box, intrigued by mention of his bomb shelter. He took secret pride in its construction, twice the size of any he had studied in blueprints and models made available through his military connections. If indeed there was need for such an underground dwelling, he wanted it to be as comfortable as humanly possible without spending a lifetime planning and building it. Yet he never considered actually living in it.

"What's that, Pumpkin?" He wanted to hear out her plan.

"Well, I've been thinking. Why don't we fix up a Christmas room, I mean a real Christmas room, the way it used to be?"

"We have our Christmas room, dear. Why do you think we need another?" Miriam was growing tired of the resistance but knew the only way to end the old argument was to entertain the renewed argument and bring it to its conclusion.

"Okay, so my Christmas present will be my own Christmas room. Is that too much to ask? I mean it's already there. I can just fix it up with all my decorations. The only thing I'd like is possibly a TV set up. What do you think, Dad? It would really mean a lot to me."

And so ended the nascent argument, for the devoted dad could not resist the gentle pleadings of his little girl. "It's not such a bad idea, Mir. It might be a fun project."

Mir or Miriam picked up her ballpoint pen and jotted a few more notes on the lined paper, which included ingredients for a new cookie recipe using maraschino cherries, coconut extract, and chocolate chip morsels. She had lost the final battle, her only consolation being a sparkling tree exactly where she wanted, her tin-like trophy of consumer desire.

* * *

Lori and her dad connected on a new level with the Christmas room project. She warily eyed him setting up a television set, wondering how in the world he would be able to get any reception. Then it happened. The fuzzy image became crystal clear while she sorted through boxes. There against the far right side of her shoebox-shaped space gleamed a picture of a heart with "I Love Lucy" slowly appearing in the center as bongo drums and a catchy tune sent a glee-like thrill lifting her attitude from feelings of uncertainty to a new high. Elevated by the success, she beamed a smile brighter than the picture tube itself. Her dad, feeling the heat of accomplishment, checked the dial and confirmed what he already had deduced. "Only one channel, Pumpkin. That's all I can get."

"I'm okay with it, Dad. It'll keep me company while I unpack. Thanks for the best Christmas present ever!" She wasn't sure she meant it, but she knew in her heart he deserved it: the gratitude so often unspoken.

The invincible Lucy and her accomplice Ethel, in the midst of a madcap escapade, provided light in the unlighted space and kept Lori company as she unpacked layer after layer of ornament boxes. The evergreen tree arrived an hour earlier, compliments of the tree lot assistant who served as the delivery boy. Cognizant of the special wish, Grandma Mitchell had ordered a soft-needled Douglas fir, just big enough to fit through the opening and down the stairs with ease. Attached to a cotton velvet crimson bow was a personalized card, "Merry Christmas, Lori." Shaking out a shaggy, loose-loomed ivory rug with a fern green border, Lori placed it next to the miniature-sized tree. She knelt down and closely examined a sampling of her prized collection. Digging deep into the bottom of a storage bin beneath ornament boxes and elves and angels wrapped in sparkled tissue paper, Lori cupped her favorite new heirloom.

Two years ago, Grandma Mitchell gifted her with an ornate little statue she called the Infant of Prague. Intrigued by the boy in royal robes, gold-trimmed and hand-sewn by an Irish woman name Bridget in Boston, Lori placed it on her dresser for an entire year before reluctantly packing it away for the following December. Now she had a new home for it, at least until Christmas was rightfully restored to the Hopkins household. A corner table of rich mahogany that no longer matched her mother's decor made its way to Lori's new enclave and the temporary throne for her personal prince. Nothing gave her more peace than thoughts of the boy Savior. She pressed the form against her heart before relinquishing the statue to its new, if not regal, setting. Now she could recite the St. Andrew's prayer she learned in Sunday school at the age of ten. Never one to dwell on her faith lessons, yet for some reason, the images dazzled her with the sheer wonder of the nativity story. From November 30 through Christmas Eve, Lori would repeat the hope-filled, gentle words fifteen times each day. "Hail and blessed be the hour and moment in which the Son of God was born of the most pure Virgin Mary, at midnight, in Bethlehem, in piercing cold. In that hour, vouchsafe, O my God! to hear my prayer and grant my desires, through the merits of Our Saviour Jesus Christ, and of His Blessed Mother. Amen."

Lori glanced over at the oversized shrub and reflected charitably on Grandma Mitchell who only wanted harmony with the world within her family. She served as buffer between daughter and granddaughter on too many occasions. Lori felt a pang of guilt for vexing a stately woman filled with love and compassion. She imagined her like Florence Nightingale tending to wounded warriors in dimly lit makeshift hospital wards with canvas for walls and hardened dirt for floors. She frequently thought her grandmother was too unkind to herself carrying the burden of some unnamed cross on her shoulders. Could she take full blame for her daughter's insecurities? Miriam Mitchell Hopkins had a nervous condition, even if unnamed, that manifested itself in her quirky obsessions. Simply put, she was neurotic, and Lori was convinced it had nothing to do with scars from formative years or anything related to her upbringing. It's just who she was, and no one needed to take responsibility, especially Grandma Mitchell.

The panic of nuclear obliteration only fed her fragile mother's neuroses placated by the latest fashions and fads. Hence, the tree dilemma. Hence, the button swiping. Hence, Lori's vague sense of remorse for punishing a woman so vulnerable to wearing every weakness on her sleeve with or without buttons. But life was looking better, yes, exuberant in her bastion of holiday bliss. Even in the dankness of cinder blocks, the bleakness was lifted by unboxing and rediscovering treasured memories in her relatively short life.

On Sunday, before winter vacation, she would invite Joy to step down into her world and share a cup of hot cocoa with marshmallows and a plate of shaped sugar cookies iced to perfection, Mexican wedding cakes—soft and powdery—and molasses crisps that looked like coffee-colored lace. Even though her mom was a tree traitor, she held on to the baking traditions that previously had mother and daughter joining hands over mixing bowls and cookie sheets. This year, Lori held out and let her mom orchestrate the kitchen projects on her own. Her sulking, silence, and absence were the final remonstrations of protest. Yet in the forced ugliness of the standoff, Lori was already letting go of harbored hurts. The plan was to make peace on Christmas Day with a beautiful new sweater purchased with a year's worth of saved allowance. It was a soft rose pink of angora with pearly white buttons. Along with the carefully wrapped gift, she would include the box of missing buttons with the most sincere apology ever uttered by a recalcitrant yet penitent offspring. Lori carefully affixed her angel ornament on the tree top. The sweet, smiling face looked down on her as if anointing her private place. In the background, Lucy and Ethel were doing what they do best, plotting and scheming, and this time, it was how to join Ricky and his band on a European tour. Clasping her hands, Lori said a silent prayer of gratitude and settled in to watch her favorite television show.

6

Buttons and Bows

Larry and Fran abandoned any interest in the time capsule, expending all of their curiosity in two visits. Alone in the bunker, Peggy sorted through small neatly wrapped packages stacked under the tree. One in particular, decorated with buttons and bows, caught her eye. It was round like a small hat box, the size of her palm. She lifted open the top and shook the array of loose buttons of every sort and size, hardly two alike. She opened the small loose leaf note tucked inside and read it aloud: "Merry Christmas, Mom, I am sorry it has taken me three years to return your lost buttons. I hope you enjoy them once again and please forgive me for not returning them sooner. Love, Lori."

Peggy examined a button the size and look of a real pearl, and a young voice sounded out as if from the very walls of the ornamented fortress. "No, don't lose that one please. It's the first."

Peggy froze. Someone else had infiltrated the long-forgotten hideaway. She wondered if that someone had followed her and wished desperately for a weapon. Scanning the room for a sharp object, Peggy answered back.

"The first what?" Her eyes darted back and forth across the cement box, searching for the mischief maker.

"The first button I hid," said the voice in a somber, almost apologetic, tone.

"Why? Why would you do that?" Peggy eyed her surroundings with renewed astonishment as she carried on a conversation with an unseen intruder. She waited for a reply, but the walls fell silent with Peggy's doubts filling the empty space. Sorting through the box of buttons again, she chose a large, shiny black one. The voice returned.

"That one broke her heart."

With a final glance, Peggy despaired of encountering any manifestation, whether real or imagined. Suddenly, she was seized by a notion of how to expose the vexing observer. "Well, I need to go." Peggy cradled the gift box while circling the room.

"Don't leave!" An urgent plea bounced from the walls. "You have my buttons!"

Emboldened by a plan, Peggy gave off an insouciant air and sly grin. "Oh yeah." Walking slowly to the adorned tree, she stooped down and leaned inward, searching for a place to drop the box. With a jolt, she shot back up and announced, "You know, on second thought, I just might use these. Who doesn't need a spare button every now and then?" Holding the little treasure box like a trophy, she added nonchalantly, "Thanks!" Tucking the box under her arm, Peggy strode jauntily toward the steps leading outside.

"No, wait. You can't take the buttons! I need to return them!"

Peggy's frustration hit her own interior wall, and she felt the urge to dash out of the time capsule with the echoing voice. "No, I'm going." She moved closer to the steps. She had no inclination to lift any other items from the room, even if they would sell for a few dollars. The only other novelty that attracted her attention was sitting next to a nativity set with the worn look of a family heirloom. Peggy noted that tucked away on a polished wooden table was a statue of a small child wearing royal robes. His head was capped with light brown curls and adorned with an extravagantly jeweled crown, a gold cross at its apex. In one hand, the child held a blue orb. The other small hand held two fingers raised as a sign of peace. Peggy briefly considered pocketing it and surprising her mother. She assumed it to be a Christ figure although she did not recall any likenesses other than an infant cradled in a rough manger or a bearded man hanging from a cross.

"I really think I could use these buttons," she said, peering into the shadowy room.

"No, I won't allow you to take them," the voice sounded more pleading than threatening.

Peggy felt brave and reckless all at once. Nothing or no one materialized, only a voice. The persistent, pleading, and eerie voice of a girl, a young teen. Peggy pushed on with an uncanny sense of reaching across a hidden dimension. In a flash, a beaming, freckle-faced Lori observed an ashen Peggy clutching the mini hatbox. The materialized Lori studied her own hand as it extended outward to reclaim the purloined buttons.

"Who are you? What are you?" stammered Peggy in a blended state of disbelieving shock and total amazement. Only half of Lori's torso and extremities were visible. Peggy dropped the cylindrical package, allowing it to roll across the floor. "I must be dreaming." She gazed open-mouthed at the half-emerged vision of a quirky teenager.

"Oh, no!" Lori watched the buttons roll around on the cement floor covered only with a few bits of green carpet.

In a frantic chase, Lori jumped to the task in full flesh from behind an invisible curtain of time and space. Her honey-colored hair, pulled behind in a ponytail, bobbed back and forth as she searched for every last colored piece of plastic quickly spinning and spreading over the barricade floor.

"This is a game, right? Okay, who put you up to this, huh?" Peggy folded her arms tightly across her denim jacket, the stance of a night guardsman stumbling across a suspicious loiterer.

What took place next was so extraordinary that Peggy pinched herself to make sure she hadn't entered a chronic dream state.

Lori glanced up. She had managed to recapture every button, each one a bitter reminder of shameful childish antics. With a toss of her head, she stretched out a hand. "Hi, I'm Lori. Are you new in town?"

7

Stealing Glances

Peggy stood, speechless. She sized up the bouncy figure and quickly sorted through a mental list of culprits for such an outlandish hoax. Possibly one of her many siblings created the ultimate con game. How could she be so deceived by amateurs? She was the master of trickery, and now she was dealt a trump card.

"So who put you up to this?" She gave her best glare, hoping it would work like a truth serum.

Lori smiled bemusedly. "Well, it was actually my mom. She wasn't keen on me using our bomb shelter here, and now I'm sort of stuck with no way out. Did you come to help me?"

Peggy shook her head slowly and returned the smile resigned to playing out the con game. "Okay, well, let me show you the way out."

"Oh, I know the way out," beamed Lori.

Suddenly annoyed by the charade, Peggy chortled, "Are you sure? You've been here for what sixty years now, right? Do you think maybe you would have found your way out by now?"

Lori pondered the sharp accusatory words from the decidedly unkind stranger. The young lady had an edge about her Lori never encountered in her world of friends, schoolmates, and family. "I can't seem to open the door. It must be stuck. I've yelled and yelled, but no one hears me."

Peggy was increasingly perplexed. "Wait a minute. How long have you been in here?" An unblinking Peggy continued, "What's today's date?"

Lori batted her eyes to clear her thoughts. "It's December 19."

"Year, I mean what year?" Peggy heard an answer already echoing in her mind.

Lori glared at her intruder with the same disbelief. Who was this excitable teen with her speculations? Squinting her eyes in deep thought, she spun around her underground cocoon. Giving a quick shoulder shrug, she pointed at the festive chalkboard. She couldn't say the words. All she could manage was "Right?" and their worlds fused, collided, blended into a total sense of life's mysteries, especially—and notably—*time.*

Peggy cleared her throat and peered straight into the girl's confused eyes. "How long did you say you've been here?" She needed a recanting of facts that defied the present logic.

"In here?" Lori fancied herself on a witness stand. "I said it's only been a few hours. The door is stuck, so I'm glad you found your way in."

A clarifying moment arrived for a reeling Peggy. If the vision was merely a figment, a result of oxygen deprivation, light-headedness, or some dream state, it would certainly vanish in the real world outside of a murky cave. "No problem, I'll get us out of here." Peggy breathed in the disturbing air and headed toward the steps.

"I think I'll leave my buttons behind. Christmas is only days away." Lori leaned over, placing her stash of purloined buttons in their former place under the tree. Peggy studied the subject of her mental confusion and decided immediately to dismiss her once again as a prankster. Must be one of my vengeful siblings, she mulled over, knowing full well she was deserving of anything they would dish out.

"All right then, let's go."

Up the stairs they went into the brilliant sun and harsh stinging air of a Texas winter. The light of day did nothing to diminish Peggy's suspicions. For now, she had proof that the girl who called herself Lori was indeed flesh and bones. Lori's reaction to her unearthing was a different story. Stepping out into the wide open space, she backed away and shoved Peggy in fear.

"What sort of joke is this? Where's my house?" She twirled around, mouth agape. "Where's my house? This isn't my home."

Real horror and shock was a reaction familiar to Peggy. Her weekend in a detention center shook her to the depths of her being, even if it didn't result in a conversion or turnaround to a righteous path. And now, she observed a face paralyzed with confusion and instantly felt sorrow and empathy for what she considered a deranged mental case entrusted to her care. The wild swings of searching out truth were underway.

"Look, I don't know who you are, but it's clear you need help."

Lori gave a savage look as she circled around the deserted lot and overgrown weeds. "Did it happen then?"

"Did *what* happen?" Peggy remained incurious to the particulars of Lori's seeming machinations. She continued to believe, partly, that the elaborate hoax was planned for a forthcoming revelation.

By contrast, Lori felt a rush of awareness of the sheer uncertainty of life. "The bomb. You know, the *big one*," she replied with searching eyes.

Peggy kicked a clump of grass, sensing a detachment coming over her and a dreaded fear that the girl would cling to her like a lost and frightened pup. For a frozen moment, she rued her descent into the dark, musty space now resulting in a weight around her ankle named Lori. "How about you come home with me, and we'll figure out where to find your parents? What's your last name?"

Cheeks hot with tears, Lori faced her sanctuary with a bent head. "Hopkins. Lori Hopkins." She raised a hand to her face and wiped it dry. "Look, this is a bad dream or something. I'm going back, maybe I fell asleep. Maybe I just need to wake up."

"Okay, fine by me." Peggy's impatience, coupled with her usual lack of sanguinity, added a hopeless dimension to the circumstance. Fingers pointed to the ground, she barked, "Go back to your hole and go haunt someone else. I'm through with this goof. I don't know who put you up to this, and, personally, I don't care."

Lori glanced sideways at the paper-thin girl with boyish clothes. "You're the worst nightmare I've ever had. I don't know who you are, but you're mean and ugly."

Peggy glared back, speechless and infuriated. Without a second thought, she pushed the strangely awkward Lori who nearly lost her footing. If there's one evident flaw Peggy acknowledged, it was her quick, bad-tempered reactions. She would never possess the virtuous patience so abundantly apparent in her mother. Unfortunately, she was left with the residual sorrow for shrewlike behavior, and this occasion was no exception.

Lori rushed back down the steps with an apologetic Peggy at her heels. "Look, I'm sorry."

Back underground, Lori blinked hard and closed her eyes. "Maybe if I just fall asleep down here, you'll go away, and my house will be here. Everything will reverse."

Remorse was a given for Peggy. "Okay, like I said, I'm sorry, and I really think you should just come with me. Maybe I can explain some stuff to you."

"Stuff?" Lori was numb. Her Christmas hideaway turned bad dream had a reeling effect.

"Yeah, like what happened in the, uh, couple of hours you were down here."

In a moment of resignation, Lori succumbed to her present situation. "Okay, I give in. I'll go on one condition."

Peggy muttered to herself, "Okay, now I have conditions. This is going to be really hard." She glowered at the odd creature similar only in age and shrugged her shoulders in affirmation.

Lori inspected her shelter with wary eyes. Seconds turned to minutes in the silence of contemplation. She peered at the top of her mahogany table and the vacant spot left for the child-life figure in royal robes. "You return my infant statue to me."

Peggy's sleight of hand was legendary in her circles, but she conceded readily to this strange, haunting girl with the penetrating gaze. The exchange was brief, and the small figure was retrieved by Lori only if to make sense of her ordeal and bring comfort to bewilderment. Once again, they emerged silently and further thrown off by the confusion following them like shadows on a brightly lit day. Peggy observed Lori, nearly catatonic as she stepped along a deserted field where once neatly lined ranch homes bordered pristine paved roads. Only ten homes were built back in the midfifties, but plans were underway to extend the new development with at least five more tree-named streets. Lori walked a few more steps, dragging her brown loafers across uneven ground and blurted out a message of consternation strangely reading her new guardian's thoughts.

Arms crossed, she continued, "You know what your problem is? You think the world owes you, but I've got news for you, buster."

"Buster?" Peggy slowed her quick stride, intrigued by the sudden tirade of emotion. She dreaded making constant amends to a new source of irritation.

"That's right, buster. The world doesn't owe you anything, so why don't you stop feeling sorry for yourself and just get on with your life?" Lori adjusted her green headband and stood perfectly still.

Peggy sneered, eager for a slight battle of words. "Well, if anyone needs to get on with her life, it's you. Somewhere, you might be real and, if so, pretty old. Not here, not now." She continued her argument with the precision of a surgical knife. "So if you're real, you're outside of yourself, and I mean that in the most literal way possible."

A staring contest ensued, and words failed the bruised up boxers inside their ring of verbal jabs. "Why did you have to find me? Why couldn't you be someone kind and, uh, more like me?" Lori pouted her best pout, knowing full well it would fall upon an unsympathetic, unlikely confidante.

Peggy wanted to cry for the first time since a toddler making her way to the cookie jar only to have her hand smacked and the relished treat seized by an older sibling with the resented chore of babysitting.

"*I don't know. I don't know anything right now, and I wish you would disappear.*" She repeatedly snapped her fingers inches away from Lori's astonished look. On the fifth, furious snap, Lori sadly smiled and disappeared in the truest ever bat of an eye with an end-of-her-wits Peggy blinking furiously in return.

8

Joy-Filled Times

Lori sat in her underground parlor and waited for Joy, not the Christmas joy mere days away, but her friend and confidante. Mr. Hopkins, in every attempt to placate a disgruntled daughter, figured out a way to wire the antenna to also receive two additional television channels. He was so proud of his accomplishment that he stopped by occasionally, usually when Lori was asleep, just to make sure he didn't lose the connection. He would find Lori, curled up in an early twentieth century wing back chair that lost its prestige as the seat of honor with the new house decor. Draped across her lap was a blue and white quilt lovingly knitted by Grandma Mitchell for rainy days, snuggling sessions, and pleasant dreams.

Sensing his presence, she blinked her eyes and stretched out her lanky limbs. "Hi, Pop. Guess I dozed off. What time is it?"

"Well, Pumpkin, it's nearly three o'clock. Are you coming up for dinner? Mom's cooking one of your favorites. Chicken pot pies."

"I was asleep for an hour? Maybe I missed her. Joy was supposed to stop by at two this afternoon. Maybe she knocked, and I didn't hear her." A still sleepy Lori sat upright in the wing chair and gave off the air of a disgruntled elf surrounded by her favorite, even if unnoticed, Christmas treasures from Santa's workshop.

How easily she pouted and showed displeasure, like her mom, thought Mr. Hopkins.

They were somewhat distorted mirror images, which explained their hostility to each other. So many people disliked the traits in others they didn't easily recognize in themselves. Mr. Hopkins was a practical man, and he adored his family even though they were going through a rough year or two. Boston seemed light years away from Texas, and there were many times he yearned for his hot breath floating across the icy chill of a winter morning blanketed by glistening snow as far as the eye could see. Oh, Texas had its share of Mother Nature but, in the worst way with tornadoes, droughts, and the occasional hurricane finding land far away from its origin at the Gulf Coast. He still heard about the Great Dust Storm of twenty years ago that deepened the effects of an already-scarred nation battling the Great Depression and forcing droves of the disenfranchised westward.

"Well, why don't you give her a call and invite her over for dinner?" Mr. Hopkins checked the channels on the small console television set in the corner. Not one to pride himself too much on accomplishments, he still marveled at this one. He never, in his imagination, thought this space would really be used by his family, let alone for the catastrophic forces of a nuclear war.

"No, I don't think so. I really just wanted her to come down here. I wonder why she didn't visit."

"Well, you won't know unless you call her, Pumpkin." Mr. Hopkins checked his watch and had a sudden flashback of his siblings gathering around the Christmas tree in a Victorian parlor near Bunker Hill. Oh, how he missed them especially at this time of year, overflowing with deep sentiments and a longing for his little sister Bernadette's hot chocolate, the absolute best in New England.

Now his only connection was a long-distance "Merry Christmas" from a receiver passed around to brothers, sisters, aunts, uncles, nieces, nephews, and an occasional neighbor who popped in for eggnog. Each voice was a reminder of his absence, and he stared at his watch as if it would transport him back via a magic frosty window. Suddenly, a light rap filled the few moments of silence.

"It's Joy! She's here." Lori sprung from her half-reclining position and climbed up the stairs. Opening up the heavy door, she flashed a beckoning smile to her beloved friend. "I knew you'd be here. What happened? You're an hour late." Lori was both relieved and perturbed, feeling slightly stood up.

"My mom had a bunch of chores for me. I thought I'd never get out of the house." Joy looked a little sad, and Lori felt instantly sorry for snapping at her.

"It's okay, I guess. C'mon down before it gets really dark. I have hurricane lamps to keep the place lit. Hey, Dad, Joy and I are going to spend some time together decorating."

"More? Is there anything left?" Mr. Hopkins dug his hands into his tweed jacket and surveyed the room growing dimmer of anything but spirit with the presence of the sun diminishing outside.

"I have one more box over here." Lori walked over to a corner and dragged a cardboard box to the middle of the room. "There's just a few more ornaments for my tree. Oh, and this new garland. I bought it special for my tree." Lori gleefully opened a box, like a two-year-old, fascinated by the wrapping as well as the gift inside. "It's not real, but I thought it was pretty." She held up a long stretch of garland studded with cotton velour ruby red poinsettias with buttery yellow centers. "No tinsel this year," she added with a twinkle and wink at her father.

9

Home Sweet Home

"It's the weed," she muttered, shaking her head on a lumpy, misshapen pillow, knowing all well her last joint was nearly two weeks ago. No drugs since then, no easy blame for a bewildered state that haunted her memory.

One week had progressed since the incident. A girl, a throwback from the fifties. She entertained notions that Lori, afflicted with early onset of schizophrenia or some yet unnamed mental illness, went AWOL from some state institution and found her way into the bomb shelter. Maybe the strange girl named Lori was delusional, and when she saw the date of 1955, figured she was from the era. It didn't really matter because what really vexed Peggy was the vanishing act. *So I really did dream her up. I must have.* She knew her only way back to a road of sanity was to return with her accomplices, Fran and Larry, to the unearthly hole and hope they would also meet the deranged person. Dimness gave way to morning, and Peggy met the first streaks of dawn with the screams and cries of her youngest sibling, Miriam. Thoughts of Lori, once incessant, faded like a projected image in harsh light. Before another impression formed, a torrent of renewed wailing pierced through the walls outside her room. Yes, Miriam was in full gale force, and even though well beyond the toddler age and its taxing behavior, she was apt to seek and garner attention in the strangest ways. Peggy cushioned her head to muffle the abrading sound. Although she tolerated her family, she preferred not being in their company and spent most of her time in her bedroom hideout. She had a small bureau all to herself, packed with purloined articles.

Every now and then, she would take a few objects out to examine, whether a small comb, a superhero comic book, reminders of the challenge of lifting possessions from their rightful owner.

Peggy wasn't the person she wanted to be, and Lori, with all of her pleasantries, was obviously tormented by the buttons. She thought about the buttons. Without those little plastic discs, Peggy may have never evoked the fierce response from the deranged girl who must have been hiding in an unperceived dim corner. If only the whole episode was merely some strange dream in a long night of REM sequences. Meanwhile, the wailing continued, and she waited for her mother to investigate the matter. She envied her older siblings, Mark, Matthew, Matilda, and the first set of twins, Maria and Monica, all headed out into the world on divergent paths. Mark, twenty-five, and Matthew, twenty-three, were living together in Dallas as recent college graduates. Mark, the family techno-geek, as Peggy refers to him, graduated from the University of Texas in computer engineering and secured a job writing software for a financial company. Matthew, the most creative of all the Mitchells, pursued culinary arts and left Lubbock for the Sorbonne in Paris. How he got there, no one really knows, but he returned to Texas as a master chef with a burning desire to start a gourmet catering service. Dallas seemed like the perfect place to feed people expensively, so he pleaded with Mark, a bit of a self-centered twit, to bunk with him until he got on his feet as an entrepreneur.

As far as Peggy was concerned, their arrangement must be working since no one has seen them in the last year. Mrs. Mitchell reminded them at Christmas that it was a holy day, and they promised to attend a mass to celebrate the birth of Jesus. She asked if they would mail her a copy of the church bulletin of the mass they attended, and Mark said they would be happy to oblige. Of course, anyone in his or her right mind knew they could slip into a place of worship and take one of the weekly publications, but that didn't bother Mary Mitchell. As long as they passed through the doors, there was some opportunity for conversion. Matilda, now twenty, was considered the lost party of one in the family and doomed to hate her name until her dying breath. The rest of the kids called her Tilda, which riled her further; but Sister Gertrude, a wise old nun, told her that we are called by name before we're born, which made her question why God would be so mean. As a teenager, her method of anger management was to run away on a regular basis, which just made a lame statement because she really didn't run away. A few days into her absence, Mary Mitchell would get a phone call from a friend's parent, saying, "It was nice to have Tilda with us for the weekend. Would you like to pick her up? If not, we'd be delighted to drive her home." Most likely, the parent expressed some form of gleeful relief because Tilda, or Matilda as Peggy called her, had a way of unnerving the calmest creature after about half-a-day. Once comfortable in an environment, she felt called to engage in mischief by some odd sense of vindication, which she blamed on her name.

The worst sampling of her antics happened on a Fourth of July weekend when, as expected, Tilda took off with a friend's family claiming total assurance that it was absolutely fine for her to join them on a road trip to Galveston Bay. She crafted a meticulously handwritten note from her mother, explaining that her father traveled as a trucker and dear old mom had a month-old case of laryngitis. So Tilda, a fifteen-year-old minor, was gone for five days. Mary Mitchell was worried sick over her missing daughter even though all the other kids consoled her that she was with a friend and convinced her not to call the police. Plus, it was her modus operandi to disappear for days at a time with neighboring families. No one was ever surprised by her disappearance, and actually, greatly anticipated her absences. In this instance, Tilda initiated a preholiday show not realizing that fireworks needed clearance from yards and combustible structures, especially the host's house. A tiny spark flew off an ascending starlike shoot and, with a small blaze, ignited a section of the wood-framed closed-in porch.

The local fire company was plenty busy that evening, with all sorts of holiday calamities, but none as embarrassing as the scorched porch incident. Tilda's host family left their bay house earlier than scheduled and dropped off a slightly remorseful Tilda to the awaiting arms of the ever-loving Mary Mitchell who held up hope for all her children, especially the vagarious runaway. Years later, after she barely eked out a high school diploma, Tilda, Matilda, or Matte—as referred to by her newly found college friends—relocated to Machu Piccu, Peru, with a research team studying diminishing forestry in the tropics. The only Matilda reminder for her family in Texas was a map of Australia recalling the continent associated with her name. Maybe it was the large print, studied year after year by a non-waltzing Matilda, that drew her into seeking remote regions of the Lone Star state and escaping ordinary, everyday family life.

Maria and Monica, brilliant at everything, relocated to Washington DC in their first year of college at Catholic University. They were the only two Mitchells that embraced the religious fervor so incessantly promoted by a long-suffering family matron. At home, Peggy breathed easier sans wall-to-wall Mitchells, despite the bothersome antics of the youngest of the brood. A precocious child with a capital P, Miriam knew how to stir the family pot of accusations and turmoil with a self-willed impudence. Her piercing screams were a legend in the making whether a simple squeal of joy or the quick display of a budding temper. No one, not even the intuitive Mary, could predict the outbursts and what incident would set her off. This morning, Miriam was certain she saw a terrifying shadow.

10

Santa Baby

Lori slept soundly, albeit no visions of sugarplums dancing across her cerebral cortex. Joy had only spent a half-hour in the Christmas room, feeling a little unnerved at being underground, like being buried alive. She spoke incessantly of the upcoming school holiday dance with the hottest new act to hit the music scene. Undecided about the poodle skirt, Joy described other possible outfits for review and comment. Lori, only mildly interested in the dance, said she'd prefer to spend the evening listening to Christmas songs and pointed to a stack of records she had that were waiting for a spin. Her favorite at the moment was the cooing siren Eartha Kitt coquettishly warbling and enticing Santa to put diamonds, furs, and a new car under her tree. She hugged Joy good-bye and offered her a candy cane. In turn, Joy said she'd call tomorrow for a pickup time. Her dad was offering to ride them to the dance and, of course, pick them up at a reasonable hour. Lori nodded in agreement and said she'd probably go, if only to watch the awkward moments between teachers who seemed to like each other but were watching their Ps and Qs in public spaces.

As if reading her thoughts, Joy gave an impish grin, "You'd go if Mr. Dugan was there."

"Why do you say that?" Lori perked up for the first time during the visit.

"I don't know, maybe it's that dreamy look in your eyes every time we leave his classroom." Joy had a way of imitating and acting out any scenario she committed to a statement, and there she was clasping hands under chin and batting her fringe of sable brown eyelashes in every attempt to look in love.

"That's daydreaming, silly. I'm just trying to survive his class. It's all stuff I'm not interested in."

Joy leaned forward from the small footstool she crouched on. "What does interest you these days? You don't want to go to the dance. I mean you say you'll go, but it's like you're only going because I keep bugging you about it." Joy was testing her dear friend, probing a bit, because she missed the liveliness of her self-proclaimed confidante.

"I just need to make peace with my mom. Spending time down here has made me realize it even more. It's like an awakening."

"Then what are you waiting for?" Joy was puzzled by her best friend's intentional paralysis in ending her quarrelsome ways that dragged her down into the furnished pit.

"I'm waiting for Christmas," replied Lori with a modicum of cheer. "It will have more meaning."

Joy checked her watch a second time as she felt the room grow colder and dank matched by the setting sun and night shadows above the underground sitting room. She cradled her arms rocking back and forth on the stool not sure what to say next. "Well, okay I've decided on the poodle skirt for the dance. Have you given any thought to what you're wearing? The dance is this Thursday, you know, only four nights away."

"Oh, I'll figure something out. Who am I going to impress, anyway?" Lori had a way of dismissing a conversation like an exotic queen waving away a young servant girl leaving behind a plate of figs as she bows incessantly before her exit.

As Joy bounded back up the stairs to lift the slanted door, she peeked down the steps again. "It looks fab, Lori, really fab. Don't stay down here too long though." She gave a little shiver as if to shake off the unwanted notion of being under the earth.

"Joy!" Lori heard her own plea, not sure why she called out her friend's name, only knowing the visit seemed rushed, almost perfunctory.

Joy reappeared midstep, leaning over, expectant and waiting.

A notion came to Lori as she swiftly took stock of her milieu. "I want to give you something." Bent slightly forward, she picked up a box and presented the newly purchased garland. "Here."

"You know I'm Jewish, right?" Charmed and surprised, Joy accepted the open box holding a string of pointy red petals.

"Wrap it around your Hanukah bush?" Lori gave a tilt of her head and a shy smile. Both, in their heart of hearts, knew the truth. The garland was a peace offering.

Joy hugged her friend in a clumsy embrace, giggling at her own awkwardness.

"Maybe I'll drape it around Elvis after the dance!" she added with a chuckle.

Hands cradling her head, Lori winced. "Only if you want to scare him away. Okay, even I'll stay to see that one!"

"Deal! Now I've really got to go!" Joy lifted the door once again and vanished.

Lori didn't expect Joy or anyone else to understand her room of treasures. She needed more than wanted these outward signs, mementos of Christmas past, her last bastion of childhood. No one would rob her of it, not even a mother immune to her pleadings of all things held dear. She settled into the rocker with a smile and intimate regard for her Infant of Prague.

11

Father Knows Best

Fran sat on the edge of Peggy's bed, head dropped down. He stared at the pink shag carpet so unstylish and matted down. Peggy had worn a pathway from her constant pacing, and he wondered what distressing thoughts kept her preoccupied. She seemed more on edge these days as if a caffeine drip was taped to her forearm. For several minutes now, he pondered the news of a strange ghostlike yet flesh-and-blood teenage girl who descended upon Peggy in a whimsical fashion. His catalogue of facts and figures didn't quite match up for any sort of logical summation. Studying the carpet, he counted careless spills and spots. Suddenly, a sharp notion pierced his considerable intellect. He knew he'd have to build his case adroitly with a doubting jury of one. Peggy ceased her march back and forth and fixed her eyes on the ceiling. "So what is it?"

Fran refolded his hands, cleared his throat, and proceeded with his argument. "Well, I'm not sure. As I said, it doesn't sound like an umbra."

"Umbra?" Peggy cocked her head and mimicked his folded arms. "Why are you throwing all those big words at me again?" She felt the heat of repressed anxiety coursing through her neck and forearms.

"Yes, umbra. A phantom or shadowy apparition. Like someone not physically present." Fran closed his eyes and waved his arms frantically swatting at an unseen being.

"Oh, you mean like a ghost? Why don't you just say ghost?" she replied matter of fact. "No, nothing like a ghost. She even has a shadow." Sitting cross-legged, Peggy cupped her chin and looked straight ahead. A wistful sigh completed her brief chronicle.

Fran stroked his chin like a lab professor devising a new scientific hypothesis. "But no one else can see her."

Peggy dropped to the floor and crossed her ankles, sensing the energy drain from her limbs. "No." She kept silent on the nagging suspicion that her little sister knew of the house visitor. But would either the intruding ghost or latest victim admit to anything?

Hands clasped, Fran now assumed the posture of a soul-searching confessor. "Where is she now?"

With a faraway gaze, she catalogued her scarce sightings in a matter of seconds. "I don't know. Sometimes, I call her and she's right there."

Fran gave a quick jolt, spreading a shock of hair along his forehead. He sorted the bits of information and blurted out an inspired hunch. "So she only chooses to appear to you. I can only think of one possibility then. Bilocation."

Peggy grabbed at the sparse fibers of her shag carpet. "Bi what?"

Fran pushed back his fringe of hair. "Bilocation. She's in two places at once."

"You totally lost me, dude."

"I know very little about it. But I know someone who can explain the whole phenomenon."

Peggy jumped to her feet, an adrenaline surge replacing the lassitude brought about by an incessantly muddled state. "Okay, lead the way, my friend."

* * *

The rectory door with its old-fashioned brass knocker was symbolic of a last resort for Peggy. She rarely visited the parish church, let alone the parish priest. Mary Mitchell tired of the constant battling of an overly reluctant child resistant to attending any liturgies. Hence, she left Peggy home since the age of thirteen, a few years beyond the age of reason. The distraught family matron would say an entire rosary for her daughter's conversion on the way to mass, towing along all the other Mitchell children and, sporadically, a few neighboring kids whose parents were not yet awake on a Sunday morning. All in all, she usually toted a dozen or so children through the front doors with just about every head turned in her direction as they marched up the aisle. A spectacle for some, she recalled one new parishioner, during the monthly social, asking her if she ran an orphanage, which made Mary laugh until she cried leaving the sorry inquisitor more than slightly embarrassed.

Peggy and Fran were led into a parlor area with musty, weighty furniture and worn braided, oval rugs. Mahogany shelves of thick, heavy, leather-bound books lined the walls adding to the room's esoteric quality. Joan Speakman, the parish secretary, pursed her already thin lips and tucked a stray hairpin back in her mousy bun. Her pink sweater matched the ruddiness of her complexion, and she appeared dubious of the impromptu visitors' intentions yet resigned to fulfill the obligation of announcing their arrival.

"Well I guess you're in luck because Father Norton is still here. He'll be leaving in a few hours for the mission church, but he likes to be spontaneous as he's told me on several occasions and not to turn any visitors away if he's here, no matter what he's doing, so I'll go tell him you're here."

Peggy wondered how the woman could speak an entire proclamation without taking a breath. A few moments of blissful silence and Father Norton was heading in their direction with quick strides. Peggy remembered him from mass, although she rarely listened to a word he uttered and only peeped at him through a rolled up bulletin when ushered into a pew for what seemed an interminable period of time. Now she was up close and personal and instantly noted his kind countenance and admired the theatrical quality to his voice. A cheerful greeter, he offered a hearty handshake and extended arms signaling his visitors to resume their seats.

"So, Fran, I haven't seen you for a few weeks. What's going on? You look familiar too."

"Hi, Father Norton. Yeah, I've been meaning to go to confession, but you know how it is."

Father Norton noted a steely-eyed Peggy. "So what's the visit about," he replied, plopping down on a nearby oxblood leather recliner.

"Well, my friend here, Peggy, she's having some sort of supernatural experience or something." Fran directed his attention to Peggy.

"What's going on?" Father Norton leaned a little forward.

Peggy shot up and began pacing. "There's really not much to tell, so this won't take long."

Father Norton checked his wrist watch. "I have an hour."

Peggy continued pacing. "Like I said, this won't take long. I have a ghost or something. I don't know what she is actually. I found her in an old bomb shelter. But she's not always there. Sometimes, she's with me, and sometimes, she just disappears. No one else can see her."

Father Norton leaned back with a thoughtful demeanor. "Does she have a name?"

"Lori. She lived there. I mean in the house that's no longer there, but she thinks it's still December 1955, and that she's been in this bomb shelter for only a couple hours. She's my age. Fourteen."

"Well, this is beyond my priestly knowledge of the supernatural. I think you've stumbled across an amnesia victim." Father Nolan stroked his clean-shaven chin, an ingrained habit from years of donning a beard more recently made unbearable due to the Texas summer months.

Fran interjected, "You forgot one important thing. She disappears, and no one else has seen her but Peggy."

"Yes, yes, I understand." Father Norton studied his young storyteller. Very slight of build with an angry aura. Sadness and guilt too. Lonely, maybe lonely enough to invent an imaginary companion. He decided to go for it. "My dear Peggy. Is it at all possible that you've dreamt up this person?" Father Norton waited only a few seconds for the reaction he anticipated.

Peggy shot up like a firecracker. "See, I told you he wouldn't believe me! I'm outta here." Peggy strode across the room with Fran playing interference.

"I have another theory, merely conjecture though," Father Norton bellowed in his best stage voice, and Peggy was once again caught up in the authoritative tone. "Are you willing to listen to me? It only came to me just now."

Peggy stood in the middle of the room, a stone pillar of doubt, confusion, and false bravado. Her life was crumbling around her, and she hated what she'd become since moving to Texas. She wanted to run, scream, tear down the street, and show the world the guilt scorching her insides. Father Norton could see through her like transparent tissue paper. He'd met many, many troubled teens in his fifteen years of priesthood. He'd seen misguided, misdirected ire ooze out of every pore of adjudicated youth or foster children aging out of the system, but couldn't quite get this hostile young lady from a seemingly good upbringing, opposed to many innocents damaged by abandonment, poverty, hopelessness, and abuse. Of course, he didn't know her background. He was only assuming that she had a loving home. He'd seen emotional scurrility in the best of families, and he guessed she had a rebellious nature.

He would help her as much as he could in the present time and pray in the coming days. His list was growing daily of those he prayed for, especially youth, the hoped for future of the church. Her feet were planted firmly, and once he realized she wouldn't relax enough to resume her seat, he proceeded with his theory, surprising even himself with the conceivable insight into the situation. "There might be another explanation. Bilocation. But this would be quite an anomaly."

"Bilocation? Yes, that's what I'm thinking." Fran was ready to embrace anything the priest said only if to allay the fears and confusion of his friend.

"Yes, it's the ability to exist simultaneously in two places. If the phenomenon is truly an incidence of bilocation, then the young lady who's appearing to you now must still be alive."

"That's impossible. She would be old by now. She thinks she's from 1955."

The stone pillar speaks again, thought Father Norton with amusement. "Which would make her about seventy-four years old today. This is not an ordinary bilocation, if there is such a thing. Many saints throughout the ages, even of modern times, only forty years or so ago, have bilocated and been documented to be at two places at once. Some thought, early in church history, these bilocators were in a trancelike state and were not aware that they had appeared in another location. I believe this is possible with your Lori."

"I'm not getting this Father." Peggy instantly softened in her attempt to reason out his fanciful notion. "Why do you think it's this bilocation?"

"Because I have no other explanation. But in this instance, it's almost as if you are experiencing the memory of someone."

"Impossible! How can I experience a memory?" She wanted to believe the priest only to have some explanation and not suspect she was losing her mind.

Father Norton sat, puzzling out his own theory. He had read so many cases of bilocation in the seminary and knew that other religions embraced the mystical phenomenon, but the Catholic church had documented instances. He drew upon his studies, trying to piece together an analysis fitting to the little bit of evidence or narration from a disbelieving and unwilling participant in this unnatural occurrence. With renewed vigor, he attempted a more in-depth explanation. "People, mainly, holy people, have been documented as appearing in two places simultaneously for many centuries. What I don't understand is how in the world the same person can be visible and present in two different time periods." He realized theories abounded, but what exactly occurs in the phenomenon of bilocation is uncertain. He had read several accounts supporting the prevailing theory suggesting that it is a projection of a double whether a solid physical form or ghostlike image. Many times, the double acts strangely and mechanically and does not acknowledge others when spoken to. Father Norton sprang up. He had several books in his library and reached for one he knew touched upon the bilocation theory. Flipping through the pages, he stopped with an index finger to guide him.

"Listen to this, although it's not a theological perspective. A pioneer psychical researcher, Frederic W. H. Myers, one of the founders of the Society for Psychical Research in England, along with others collected and studied reports of bilocation."

"Yeah, so what?" Peggy was more annoyed than bored. She felt the priest, attempting to be helpful, was missing the mark.

"Well, there's more," he continued. "The state of bilocation is commonly associated with technical remote viewing. In bilocation, the total remote viewer enters a heightened state of attention, which is split into two to allow the viewer access to two places at one time. Individuals who enter into this state often exhibit confusion, decreased eye movements, dazed states, rhythmic rhyming and tapping, memory lapses, and uncoordinated movements."

Peggy sat there, increasingly unconvinced. "She's none of those things."

"That's only one description." Father Norton was believing more and more that Lori's visitor was a case of bilocation. "There's one other thing." Father Norton leaned forward again like the quarterback huddled with his team in the last few minutes of the championship game. "I've read several books that further attempt to explain bilocation." He studied the young visitors, one totally absorbed by the train of thought, the other head tilted in a defiant manner. He proceeded anyway. "Basically, the human being—us—well, we consist of three distinct bodies: physical, astral, and spiritual. But…" Springing up, he began treading lightly across the area rug, with its tied rings of multicolored rags, gathering his thoughts. "Only the spirit is capable of dividing itself from the physical part and of traveling outside the body."

"Well, I don't believe what you're telling me now, so you might as well go on." Peggy's display of resistance was punctuated by folded arms and chin to chest, bracing herself with more unwelcome news. What she was hearing defied any inclination toward logic.

"My guess is that the present-day Lori is accomplishing this in her sleep. She is visiting the place of her childhood." Like a law professor providing a summation, he repeated plainly for his impromptu students, "I believe she is bilocating"—he paused, examining a pair of reading glasses on the table beside him—"as a younger version of herself. We must find this woman."

Peggy espied the rather young yet wizened priest with a speculative glance. Fran felt the urge to save the game plan. "This is all very strange, but why is it so important that we find her? Anyway, we know her name, so it shouldn't be that hard."

Father Tim Norton, beloved and kind parish priest, scratched at his brown crew cut and peered out from the reading glasses now balanced on his broad nose. "Some experts say, and this is supposition, that spontaneous and involuntary bilocation sometimes presages the death of the individual seen."

Fran kept it going. "I don't think I really understand all of what you're saying. Presage?"

"Simply put, your friend is dying."

12

Family Affairs

Miriam wished she had never entered Peggy's room. She had a penchant for snooping, and her older sister's drawer of stolen keepsakes was no secret. The young detective innocently thought Peggy was a collector of many toys and gadgets. Even though the drawers had locks, Peggy was not careful with the keys so easily discovered following Miriam's persistent search during feigned afternoon naps.

The one new collectible intrigued her the most: a small figure of a child with a royal crown and beautiful scarlet cape adorned with gold trim. She recalled a similar figure while in church with her mom and wondered why her sister, who never went to church, was hiding the prince-like statue in her drawer. In that moment of wondering, she reached for the stately form when a larger-than-life shadow appeared on the side wall. Miriam gave a blistering scream, flinging a balled-up sock in the great hopes of making it disappear. She was certain she peered at the shadow of a human form, but no person attached to it. Her scream was a natural reaction to such a frightening experience, and it wasn't the first time. On the initial occasion, she likened the creature to Tinkerbell from the *Peter Pan* story that the twins, Maria and Monica, would read to her at marathon bedtime sessions. The book's worn pages bore the smudgy fingerprints and dreams of a wistful child who fancied herself as a strikingly feminine Wendy in flight with the whimsical forest boy. But her eyes were not beholding a fairy tale in the last few moments, and she keenly understood the sharp distinction between her imagination and real occurrences.

Miriam shut her eyes tight and opened them quickly to blink away the fearful incarnation. With a second scream that would curdle milk, she hoped to scare the unnatural being back to invisible dimensions. Peggy rushed to the threshold of invaded quarters. She stood soldierlike, barring any passage.

"You could wake the dead with that scream."

Miriam kept silent, awaiting the inevitable interrogation. She gave her boldest, most defiant look to the only true rival for her mom's affections. Even as a detached toddler, Miriam vied for the attentions of her mom so bent on fixing Peggy. Mrs. Mitchell instinctively knew that Peggy was a lost soul, broken and isolated. She sensed it from the time a forlorn Peggy, at the age of four, witnessed her father's drinking bouts and sporadically abusive manner. Peggy soaked in sadness like a sponge, and Mary Mitchell would try to wring out the emotional damage.

"What's going on in here? Why did you scream?" Peggy possessed the patience of a cat before pouncing when attempting to draw out information. Her only weakness was her direct approach leaving the witness, in this case, unresponsive.

"I didn't scream," replied an unwavering Miriam.

Peggy refused to suffer exasperation at the hands of a sister less than half her age. "Then who did?" Peggy continued her line of questioning, any attempt to obtain a shred of evidence in support of her unreal reality.

In the last few days, Lori phased in and out of Peggy's life without regard for time and space. Still, no one else saw or heard her other than Miriam. Peggy knew intuitively. There was a glassy, overly introspective look to Miriam's icy-blue marble eyes. Snaring a straight answer from the five-year-old was close to impossible. Why the capricious Lori never appeared to both of them at the same time puzzled the already-dumbfounded teen. Later in the day, Peggy studied the twice-purloined buttons one by one, each telling their own story of evidence, each missing from a stored away piece of apparel. She pondered, *Why would anyone hide buttons intentionally?* It seemed hurtful in many ways but especially to the actual deceiver.

At sunset, Lori materialized in her accustomed attire—nutmeg brown swing skirt and neatly buttoned sweater of pine green. Peggy envisioned her as a Christmas tree come to life with its bottom trunk and top needles in balance.

"What's the deal? Why are you here, and who are you, really?" The direct approach was a limited yet reasonable option and spurred a new rant. "Okay. First of all, I don't believe you're bilocating or any such thing. I don't believe in you at all." Peggy searched her ghostly friend's expression for any hint of a reaction. Nothing but a placid smile curled Lori's mouth. Peggy concluded, "I conjured you up. I'm sick in the head and need help."

Lori gazed with astonishment at the young lady with the cruel, crooked lips and sad, limpid eyes. Most likely, her mission would soon be unearthed. *How is this possible?* Peggy thought about Father Norton's bilocation theory dreading such abstract terms—a young girl in appearance yet actually dying somewhere else at the same time, in earthly time.

13

Angel May Care

Father Joseph O'Malley, a wizened and humble priest, witnessed more changes in the Bride of Christ than he believed possible in one lifetime. From Latin to English to a closer translation of English to the former Latin, he embraced all liturgies with the vigor of a seminarian in earnest study. He also possessed a treasury of church-related stories passed down in his own generations of Irish family history. He heard of very few instances when such miracles of faith occurred, and he knew this was no exception. He carried within a catalog of remarkable experiences and striking images of his past into his present although he reluctantly spoke his furtive thoughts aloud. Only following deep meditation and contemplation of our Lord's abiding love did he ever allow for his congregation or anyone in his company, for that matter, to be privy to his thoughts or reflections.

As a young boy of eight, Father Joe prayed away a stuttering complex that left him nearly speechless, desperately attempting to form words perfectly in his mouth. His hopes were consistently dashed when the first utterances were forced out in sputters. The whole thought process constantly wore him out until he realized it was only his spoken prayers of the Our Father, Hail Mary, and Glory Be that gave him unhindered speech. But throughout those first eight years, he listened to others with little or no responses. He heard more than others who were busy hearing but not listening or absorbing the message.

Now he brought new energy to his work even though retired. He knew in his heart that God was guiding his path. How supremely touched he was by sufferings of the sick especially those with Alzheimer's disease who lived within the prison of their own tattered thoughts and broken mechanism for remembering even the simplest routines. It was in the isolation of a private room that he befriended Lori Hopkins, a woman with no friends or family to leave a kind word or smile behind during daily visiting hours. Not yet a victim of Alzheimer's, she appeared slack, depressed, with possible slight dementia coupled with deepening depression. Father O'Malley vaguely remembered Lori from his school days, her countenance nearly forgotten with time. She was a lower classmate and possessed a starry-eyed stare whether walking through hallways or engaged in a conversation with friends. He recalled thinking her freckles were a cute match to her strawberry blonde hair that curled neatly behind her well-shaped ears. How he could suddenly conjure an image from over sixty years ago rather astonished him.

Any sign of a brain ravaging disease had not yet surfaced or left a mark on Lori's delicate beauty. Her freckled cheeks of long ago appeared smooth and soft, with a few deep wrinkles around the outside corners of her mouth and eyes, the emblem of countless smiles and frowns. He saw her about a year ago while making his rounds in what he silently referred to as the hallway of the forgotten with infrequent or no visitors. The Pine Meadow Manor, an assisted living and total health-care facility, had a similar configuration on each of its five floors. There were seven units on each of the three hallways, three on the right and four on the left. Only five occupants lived on the fifth floor, the more secluded, less ambulatory residents. Father O'Malley visited three times weekly, offering communion and thanking God for a sound mind and sharp memory. It was in that instant he walked into the room of Lori Hopkins without knowing who he was visiting for the first time. A nativity set hewn of wood sat on a small table to the right of her bed. She was sound asleep with hands resting peacefully on her lap. He turned to leave, not wanting to disturb her when he heard a voice, more like a moan of "Yes?" a question beckoning him to remain.

Well, he thought, *at least she knows I'm here.* "Hello, you must be new in town," he said cheerfully, "I don't think I've met you. My name is Father O'Malley or Father Joe, and I've come to give you communion, if you like." He preferred not to be so casual about Eucharist, the heart, center, and source of sacramental life. Every dementia patient he encountered was similar and yet different. Some had a misdirected energy that surfaced in rage-filled acts, even if unaware of the fearful effects on those in their immediate path. The explosion of energy rarely bothered Father O'Malley who remained calloused since youth by the cold, hard fists of an abusive Dad who thought the rite of passage to manhood included a bloody nose and, if necessary, a broken one. As a Vietnam veteran at the first sparks of conflict, Father Joe—then a civilian to religious life—witnessed the suffering of the innocent man, woman, and child caught in war's brutal killing and ravages with unclear motives, other than survival, on both sides. Communism was the silent enemy, and he knew it in the deep places of his psyche.

He was honorably discharged from his marine battalion due to a hand grenade explosion leaving him blind in his left eye. From the moment he left the leech-infested, watery battleground, he never looked back at any of the physical or emotional pain in his life, and, more specifically, he never judged the penitent or unrepentant. War changed him but, by some healing force, for the better. With a wry grin, he would repeatedly state, "God allowed me to turn a blind eye toward the sins of others and show compassion and mercy."

As a young man, it was only a matter of time before he would join a seminary in his home state of Texas and, eventually, serve God as a Diocesan priest. A few years older than many of the other seminarians, Joseph kept his good eye focused on the Lord and the unseeing one blurred to the evils of what he considered an age rife with cultural detours toward human progress and enlightenment. He witnessed the church's changing features and garments throughout the implementation of the Vatican II Council practices within the liturgies. He cherished Latin as the fertile soil for other languages inspiring him to learn French, Portuguese, Italian,

Spanish, and Irish Gaelic to celebrate his cultural roots. He poured over the books written in generations of Celtic folklore blending supernatural truths with fantastic stories preserved in words rarely read or spoken beyond the Emerald Isle. His favorite exercise was reading a story beneath its surface to distinguish between the fairy tale elements and the hidden complexities of the heavenly creatures that oftentimes imposed themselves upon unwitting earthly creatures.

One narrative theme that intrigued him the most and confirmed his own strong belief involved the transcendence of angels possessing a seeming passport between worlds. His own guardian angel was revealed to him in a vivid dream with the empyreal name Simon written wispily with white clouds. Between the pages of yellowed parchment, a newly ordained Father Joseph O'Malley conjured images from a marvelous recounting of a particular guardian angel who took the form of a recognizable human to guide its intended one into a new life on earth. The passage from darkness to light was rarely easy for any wrongdoers, but angels are given choices as well between good and evil. Many and most heavenly incarnations are never revealed because they employ patience, allowing God to work out the pathway of one of the elect to its beatific destiny. Every now and then, most unknown and rarely recorded, an angel assigned to a mortal will take upon itself a special, grace-filled, and purposeful mission. Father O'Malley, at all times the seeker, discovered such a report disguised as a fable and tucked into a few pages of a favorite tome. The two-hundred-year-old story took place in Dublin, Ireland, involving Daniel, a young man of fourteen, working as an apprentice for a blacksmith. The lad was shoeing a high-spirited horse that suddenly reared up and came down hooves first with a potentially cranium-crushing force. The boy's angel, prescient of the danger, had already chosen the human likeness it would recreate, the old blacksmith as a little boy. Of course, the apprentice did not recognize the ten-year-old in his midst, but with every ounce of momentary and monumental force, the incarnate angel rolled a dazed, motionless Daniel out of the path of undeniable death. Only after Daniel's disclosing of the event did the master blacksmith recognize himself in the uncanny description.

Although he never spoke of it to the apprentice himself, he did tell his wife about the one identifying feature that the perpetually grateful Daniel remarked upon several times. Under his left eye, the elder blacksmith had a birthmark in the curious shape of a heart that finally faded by the age of fourteen. On first notice, it appeared like a tattooed tear giving him the look of a Harlequin clown. Only on very close inspection would a keen observer notice the two soft arches and lower point of a heart. Daniel described the birthmark in detail regarding the industrious onlooker who saved his life. When the blacksmith confided Daniel's story to his beloved spouse of thirty years, she proclaimed aloud clasping hands in prayer, "Mioruilt! Mioruilt!" How infrequently he had noticed the word *miracle* written in the text of a legendary tale.

The young Father O'Malley would read and ponder these words, resolute in thinking the woman's exclamation held deep conviction and pure faith. None of the fairy tales or folklore bore such utterances that invoked the spirit of God. They were merely unearthly imagining and creative interpretations of a world still strange and foreign to us when attempting to unveil its mysteries. An undeniable truth was evoked when a person cried "Miracle!" in utter amazement and sheer praise. Father O'Malley kept all of these stories of faith deep in his heart and the subconscious of his gray matter. Only in the last few days, possibly week, did he invoke them. The inciting incident, still fresh in his memory, occurred while visiting the callow priest who served as associate pastor in his last parish assignment. Father Norton and he regularly checked in with each other and compared their separate missions every six weeks or so, usually over a moderately tasty chicken dinner with the parish council. Even though retired from the administrative duties of parish life, Father O'Malley missed the camaraderie of like-minded and enlightened laity, giving him hope for the church's future.

Arriving twenty minutes early last Saturday night, he happened along two young people who were wrapping up a meeting with

Father Norton. From all appearances, they were making confession and getting absolution. The elder priest was hoping against hope they were protected against any sins of the flesh because he had witnessed how very difficult it was for sinners of any age to overcome that particular deadly sin. He rarely accessed technology, good or bad, because he knew it would steal time away from visiting with the faithful. He routinely preferred eye-to-eye contact and the visceral sensation of encounters to virtual images held flat on a screen. The world of growing isolation in the midst of greater communication mystified him. Many had advanced into a pitfall of despair, and like a sixth sense, he saw the stain of sins suppressing an individual's vital force. The ability to see an offense before its retelling was a special gift, and he used it propitiously to prepare the confessor for a meaningful penance. He knew just what to say at the precise moment in a confessional box to lift the contrite into the wide-open space of God's grace and mercy.

When he first laid eyes upon Peggy, he was overcome by her weight of sadness from the imprisonment of sin. Many times, he noted, depression was not clinical, although infrequently he recognized such in those with what he referred to as broken brains. He never liked the term mental illness because many illnesses can be cured, and he learned long ago that the remedy and miracle for psychosis was found in science. A broken brain could not be fixed, sad as it was, but it could be given a cast or crutch of sorts to keep it mobile in the circuitry of thought and action. But the disease of sin was palpable, and he felt it in Peggy not the dreaded carnal sin but one of thievery and coveting thy neighbors' goods. He spent twenty minutes in her company as she rationalized that she and her small band of purloiners did not ever, ever steal from individuals. All of their goods were pilfered from large manufacturers who overpriced their merchandise and would not miss a few of their wares.

Father O'Malley tried to impress upon the young, indignant lass that sin creates disease in the spirit and possessions taken from another corrupts the essence of life apart from the corporal body. Peggy said she wasn't sure she had a soul or any being other than the one she dressed, bathed, and fed on a daily basis. Apathy or lack of contriteness every time remained his greatest challenge with many seeking him as a confessor. His worst enemy was a cold heart and the unwillingness of potential penitents to allow God's light to illuminate their darkness. To doubt the existence of the soul was a sure way of allowing its destruction for the body—the flesh—was weak, frail, inconstant, and many times at war with the spirit. So many times, he saw the battle being waged between body and soul as if in the very atmosphere above humanity itself. Getting a clear, moral message through to the young and defiant was usually unsuccessful.

Their unrepentant inclinations, he thought, *are burdened not only with too many layers of cultural waste, like a poisoned landfill, but a reluctant heart, if not ultimately hardened.*

In Peggy, Father O'Malley saw a reluctant heart that preferred not to trust in the saving power and infinite mercy of a God made visible. He recalled her summation of the young girl named Lori and put the pieces together so quickly in his mind that it made him tremble with numinous alacrity. The story of the guardian angel long ago that appeared as a nonthreatening, friendly saving force filled his conscious mind only and fastened itself to a modern-day version of what was happening to Peggy.

It's very possible in the realm above disbelief, in the surreal world of God's kingdom that Peggy's guardian angel was leading her to the unfortunate soul in front of him at this moment. Why then would the heavenly creature take upon the demeanor and likeness of a fourteen-year-old from sixty years ago? There's a connection here, but he knew he must tread carefully for disbelief and skepticism was the reigning and dominating force of a world gone distant and cold as a frozen tundra. Divine acts were oftentimes relegated into the realm of the paranormal and random, freakish means to frighten people. Were miracles from God so far from the collective reasoning of this world when they occur daily? Every canonized saint had at least two documented miracles, and there are at least ten thousand recorded saints, who verify twenty thousand miracles of healing at a minimum. Instant acts of God were easier to comprehend with their wonder and swiftness. But the thought of angels inhabiting the earth, although popular and recounted over the centuries, remained too mysterious, even for the ever faithful.

He looked again at Lori Hopkins and saw the happy, sad girl of sixty years ago, so deftly described by a happy, sad Peggy. The similarity of dispositions was remarkable, but the innocence of the former one was palpable. Of course, everyone seemed more innocent in the context of so many years in between. Technology had advanced to the point where social media, news media, and the sheer deluge of information kept waves of truculent and rapacious trash spilling over itself endlessly. Not that all media was bad, just most of it. But maybe, just maybe, these two misses had more in common in the depths of their psyche than he would obviously be cognizant of, even with his almost supernatural ability to see into the vital force of a human soul.

But Peggy was an unconfessed, unabashed stealer, which he lamented. Never before had he wished someone to be caught in the act of theft as he did this young delinquent, hoping she would show some modicum of contriteness. He looked at her as the ringleader for the broken and lost sheep, Fran and Larry. He believed wholeheartedly they would clean up beautifully once detoured off a contorted and dimmed path of deception and maleficence. Maybe, just maybe, Lori was a light, the path of light as a guardian angel would be in this instance. The woman with gray hair and shimmers of red gold from former days spoke up from the silence. "Do I know you?"

14

Vitamin Therapy

At first it was fun and endlessly fascinating. The oohs, the aahs, the perfectly rounded mouth agape with expressions of utter surprise. The show-and-tell syndrome started with the iPad and what Lori perceived as a portable television set with itty-bitty images. She repeatedly pondered a world with no encyclopedia books, actually no books for that matter, with every piece of information available on small electronic devices.

"But the print is so teensy. I don't like it. Don't you miss turning the pages of a book?" It was only the beginning. For Lori, everything electronic seemed like a dispensable toy.

"You catch on quickly. People have an unquenchable thirst for gadgetry," Peggy smirked.

"Hmm, I guess it's human nature, huh? I mean even in my time, people were watching TV like every waking moment. Now I guess they stare into these smaller screens with no wires."

Then would come another thought flash and mouth wide enough for a fly to explore. "That's the part I don't understand. You don't plug that tiny TV into anything, and it just turns on. How? I just don't get it."

"You know what? I don't get the whole wireless thing either. I just know it works." Then came the relentless questioning and the tiresome explorations of notions and ideas that, in Peggy's mind, should have remained silent speculations. And it continued with rapid-fire questions and one word replies.

Lori: "Is it like radio waves?"

Peggy: "Yes."

Lori: "So that's what makes it work?"

Peggy: "Yes."

Lori: "Wouldn't that be like stepping back in time?"

Peggy: "No."

Lori: "So it's not really like radio waves?"

Peggy: "No."

A conversation could easily circle back to the original question with a completely opposite conclusion.

Lori sighed a lot. It was her favorite coping mechanism. Peggy was endlessly putting her to the test in her own version of a naked, blaring light bulb in a dingy room.

"If you're real, why don't you ever eat? I mean, don't you get hungry?"

Lori sighed once again and scratched her head. "I don't know if I get hungry. It's like every minute just repeats itself, so I'm permanently in the present. Do you have any food? Maybe I could try some."

Peggy dug deep into the left pocket of her denim jacket where she kept a half empty bag of M&M candies. She pulled it out and shook a few into her palm.

"M&M candies!" Lori held out her right hand. Peggy let a few colorfully coated discs drop from their wrapping. Lori stared down at the M&Ms and declared, "The milk chocolate melts in your mouth, not in your hands."

"Hey, how did you know that?" Lori giggled, increasingly intrigued by Peggy's outbursts and fiery reactions.

"M&M's have been around since before I was born, silly. A new type just came out last year. Peanut M&M's. Have you tried them?"

"There's not a candy in the world I haven't tried. Okay, so are you going to eat these or what?" Peggy's fuse was shortening.

Lori inspected the little candies in her hand. "They look like buttons, don't they?"

Oh, the cursed word, the *button* word that stopped the world for the specter! Peggy sensed another obstruction in her endless search for clues in solving her private mystery, and she'd never observed Lori eat a morsel. Yes, evidence of what she didn't know, but evidence could be gathered and sorted out later. "Yeah, maybe. So what? Who gives a rat's patootie? Just eat 'em!" Her ferocity was eternally her undoing. The enraged teen rarely adjusted to the resistance, not subjugation, of her perceived adversary. An entire minute passed in silence before Lori extended the handful of M&M's back to a defeated oppressor.

Peggy shoved the M&M's back in her pocket. She rarely, if ever, stopped doubting the existence of Lori as a frozen-in-time figure from sixty years ago. Many times, she concluded that the peculiar creature was an imposter, a girl with an axe to grind against some immaterial adversary and made Peggy the brunt of it. In turn, Lori was pleased as punch, or so she would say, to be in a world so advanced. She never dreamed of such wonders of technology and was still marveling at advances only conjured up in the science fiction of her age. Of course, these were only intermittent lapses of wonder, curiosity, and childlike enthusiasm where sorrow and confusion were the constant. The thrill surfaced at learning some further bit of information about the inherent future world. She was the proverbial candy shop purveyor. After random infusions of data, a new set of inevitable questions arose with a particular fascination for space travel. "You mean they put a man on the moon? How can that be?"

Their new hangout—since forging an off again on again, here now, and gone-in-an-instant relationship—alternated between a swing set and park bench in a shade tree area with a man-made pond harboring geese, ducks, and some midsize goldfish. Today, they sat on the park bench while Peggy read over a math problem of some inordinate complexity on her iPad. She studied the words and numbers, hoping for a solution to surface while a December chill settled in her bones.

"That's ancient history to me, poodle girl." Poodle girl was one of Peggy's several slightly derisive pet names for her unintentional new tagalong. "When did it happen?" Lori could have been a private investigator with her relentless questions one piled on top of another as she pieced together the past, present, and future. Everything beyond 1955 was held in a crystal ball existence.

"In your century, dodo brain. I was born in this century." Peggy wondered why Lori didn't take umbrage at her insulting remarks. She was inching her way to what she hoped would be a reaction, some sort of verbal attack or rise of emotions from the presumptuous investigator who quizzed her at every turn of their very twisted relationship. Lori just stood there with a faraway regard for her impudent companion. "That's right. You're fourteen, my age."

"But it's 2015, sixty years away from your time capsule!" Peggy was as insistent with her reminders of their time difference as Lori was with her interrogatories.

"Peggy? Do you believe I'm real? I'm here for a reason. How could I survive so long? It's all very confusing to me."

"Confusing to you? I'm still wondering if I'm dreaming you up! No one else sees you. It's very freaky…"

Lori, tiring easily of Peggy's disinclinations, shot up from the frosty wooden slats. "Okay, let's explore. I want to know what world events I've missed." Lori always changed the subject when Peggy went into a tirade. Her constant questions were a never-ending annoyance to a disconcerted and reluctant hostess. "I don't even know what your world looked like other than a few old TV shows."

"Oh, so you still do have television? One of the greatest inventions, huh?"

"Well as already mentioned, several times I might add, it's replaced by web TV and shows telecast from computers, iPods. Look, I will never be able to get you up to speed, even if I am stuck with you…well that is when you decide to appear." These were the moments when Peggy wanted to scream and rend her garments as she remembered hearing about biblical people when tormented by demons. The feeling would pass like a storm cloud, leaving her surprisingly peaceful and ready for further engagement, a form of surrender. Frustrated with her incomprehensible homework, Peggy switched off her iPad and addressed her park companion.

"So, bubblehead, what's your favorite TV show?"

"*I Love Lucy*. She's the best comedienne ever!" Lori gave a banner smile.

And then it happened. Lucille Ball became the bridge, an all-encompassing icon of American culture spanning the decades. Peggy, although oblivious to the world of the post-nuclear, pre-Vietnam era, was intimate with the world created by Lucy Ricardo and her sidekick Ethel. The classic vintage shows, accessed by web TV and aired on a favorite cable network, mesmerized her from the first wide-eyed close-up of the redheaded zany. Countless times, she virtually entered the small New York apartment via a computer or television screen and giggled her way through the inconceivable escapades and overt physical comedy.

"So what's your favorite episode?" Peggy, in her best deadpan look, waited for an answer, hiding her glee at the unexpected connection.

Lori gave a perplexed look. "You know Lucy? How can that be since the show is running now? I mean in my time?"

Peggy was endlessly reminded how much she had to teach or explain to her incarnation from the past. Her patience, threadbare on a good day, was surprisingly up for the challenge this time around. Taking a nice deep breath, Lori took the cue and leaned her elbows on her lap. "Hi, friends. I'm your Vitameatavegamin girl."

Peggy tried hard to resist a widening grin and contributed her part with an unblinking stare. "Are you tired, run down, listless? Do you pop out at parties? Are you unpoopular? Well are you?"

Lori continued the volley. "Yes, with Vitameatavegamin, you can spoon your way to health."

Then came the total shift of the earth's axis with the brightest smile from Peggy imaginable: teeth, crinkling eyes, and the hint of an unexercised dimple on her right cheek.

She slurred the next line in total Lucy fashion, "Mmm, it's so tasty too. Tastes just like candy."

Both girls spilled across the bench like drops of medicine on a teaspoon, reveling in the connection. Arms flailing, Lori wrapped up a magical instant. "So why don't you join all the thousands of happy, peppy people and get a great, great big bottle of vitameatavegamin tomorrow? That's vita-meata-vegamin." Lori concluded with a pronounced wink, forging a new path, a vast, open desert of new beginnings, a connection that brought stark reality to the surreal.

With a threshold crossed, a bond formed, and a moment of sheer bliss shared, Peggy experienced sparks of an innocent time in her own life. She had an awe-inspiring vision of being scrubbed down, white and gleaming with feathery wings and shimmering robes. Turning to Lori, she watched uneasily as a tear traced down her cheek and felt a pang of compassion stretching her heart and forcing her to make room for something unimaginable—real concern for another human being. Lori swiped at the lone tear and continued gazing up into a non-answering blue abyss.

"What happened to me? Why am I here?"

Peggy dropped the iPad to the ground at her feet, giving Lori her undivided attention. Even if she held no solutions, she could at least provide companionship without the resentment. "I don't know. It's a mystery. But we'll get you back to where you belong. I promise."

Lori wiped a second tear away and the beginning of a third forcefully blocking a potential stream of emotions. "And where's that?"

"Well, it's not 1955. We know that much." She gave a tremulous smile, and the two unlikely associates understood what it meant to surrender to a moment, maybe a lifetime of unquestioning faith, and a design or plan bigger than an existence created and cultivated by one's own will. "Hey, do you think you can hang out long enough for a little side trip?" Peggy had just the remedy for a sad occasion. "We're going to visit one of Lubbock's best attractions. The Buddy Holly Hall of Fame."

The biggest "oh" ever formed around Lori's lips. "Buddy Holly. I know him. He went to my high school." The sky formed threatening clouds overhead only rivaled by a furrowed brow, and a darkened, troubled flash across Lori's face. Her eyes were instantly narrowed. "And he died, didn't he? He died in a plane crash."

Peggy shook off the icy chill creeping up her spine. "Yes, he did. February 3, 1959. How could you know?"

They bore holes in each other, until Lori broke the stillness of the wintry park with a heavy, detached sigh before vanishing.

15

Sweetheart Deal

Peggy endured the poke of fingers, the slight pressure against her right eye, only to snare her oppressor. She took hold of the small offender's wrist and twisted a slight arm behind its small back.

"*Ouch*!" cried Miriam loud enough to wake an immediate past generation of Mitchells. "Why are you so mean to me?" The weightiest pout west of the Mississippi met a remorseless Peggy, tired of the constant bedevilment of the youngest sibling. She yearned for days beyond her teen years when she would be free of familial ties, perhaps visiting on holidays or occasionally dropping in for a friendly and furtive visit. Miriam keenly eyed her periodic adversary like prey wary of a circling hawk. "You steal," she blurted out unabashedly to the unsuspecting accused.

An unflinching Peggy took the comment in stride. "Anything else?" She loosened her grip on Miriam's arm and watched the incessant troublemaker rub her appendage absentmindedly while avoiding the follow up question.

"No, nothing. Why?"

"You've seen her, haven't you?" Peggy watched the expressionless face hiding the truth from her, purging thoughts and images to maintain her guise. Now Peggy was amused, so much effort on the part of the little deceiver in the presence of the self-proclaimed princess, if not queen of lies.

"I don't know what you mean, and I'm telling Mom that you twisted my arm and almost broke it."

Peggy relented. Yes, time for a sweetheart deal. "Okay, let's call a truce."

"What's that?"

Peggy, reminded that the most advanced of the Mitchells was also the youngest, switched her game plan. "I'll show you everything I have hidden here in my room."

"I've already seen everything…and your new stuff." Miriam stood her ground.

Peggy, unfazed by the brazen confession, sensed a victory. "Seeing it and possibly owning it are two different things."

"I don't believe you. You would never let me have any of your stuff."

"Why not? I don't really need any of it."

"Then why do you keep it?"

"You tell me!"

"How would I know?"

Peggy went in for another zinger. "So how many times have you seen her? Did she come in here? In my room? You know, to take it back? The doll?" Peggy's plan unfolded with every bartering word. Soon, she would have a confidante, someone to establish the shape-shifter as an aberration, an unnatural being. But for now, she would ease off.

"Look. The doll is yours 'cause I know you want it." Peggy had enough shreds of testimony from her recalcitrant informer.

"Why do you keep calling it a doll? Don't you know it's the baby Jesus like in church?"

"Of course I know that." Peggy didn't see this argument coming, but it was worth exploring, even if to rile her young sibling into an admittance of acknowledging Lori. "I can give it to you now." Peggy edged over to her bureau.

"No, I don't want it. I don't want anything from you."

Now Peggy had her edge. "You know what? I think you already took it once and brought it back. I had it face up, and now, it's facedown." Peggy peered into her drawer at the evidence.

"Maybe your friend did it."

Peggy turned slowly to face the little girl looking so panicky and perplexed.

"So when did you see her?"

Another pout and folded arms. "I'm not telling you nothin'!"

For Peggy, the nothing was everything, her confirmation complete. She immediately felt a pang of tenderness for her usual tormenter. Lori was real, in some fashion. She thought about the dueling priests and their conjectures. The heart of the matter, in Peggy's mind, was not the *what* but the unanswerable *why*?

"It's okay, pip-squeak. It's okay." She closed the bureau drawer and the topic at hand.

Miriam sat in the middle of the bed, trancelike. In a sudden surge, she confided with a torrent of words, "It's the wings that scared me the most. They're not small like the angels in my prayer book."

Peggy searched Miriam's face. "Wings?"

The youngest Mitchell appeared smaller, swallowed up by the tattered pink bedspread, knees drawn to her sharp, pointy chin, and continued, "The wings are twice her size."

16

Dueling Priests

The story pieces were fitting together even though the clergymen were seeing a different picture emerge. Father O'Malley, the revered and semiretired priest, thought through the bits of evidence and drew his final conclusion. Lori was, as he consulted in his centuries old folklore books, an angel, a guardian angel, leading a wayward Peggy away from her disastrous course. He pondered their connection while humbling himself with the realization that he did not have all the answers and, most likely, none of them. The supernatural being had taken on the form of an age mate. Someone she could relate to, just distant enough in time and space to keep Peggy wondering and searching for answers even though the perplexing drama had a share of the mystery of life itself. Father Norton, his junior colleague, was increasingly convinced that the spectral Lori was bilocating, a last attempt to make peace in this world while slipping away to the next. With the current Lori identified, he believed his case was furthered. Undoubtedly, each clergymen had notions of heavenly networking in the matter of Lori's visits.

Believing relies on faith; seeing relies on an increase of faith. Many times, it's easier to have blind faith than to reconcile evidence of one's beliefs. Father Norton knew Peggy, even if peripherally. Father O'Malley knew the young Lori she described, but only put the clues together, of course, after his serendipitous meeting of the fragile, forgotten resident of the Holly Oak assisted living complex. Father O'Malley reviewed the clues over and over in his head as if to solve a mystery or piece together a seraphic puzzle. The elder priest studied his hands, now spotted and veiny, the instruments of the sacramental table allowing God's Holy Spirit to enter into the greatest mystery imaginable, the Transubstantiation. He knew at every liturgy the exact moment it happened with the power vested in him that sprung forth from the apostolic church. Only once did he see the blood and flesh on the altar while presiding over a funeral mass for his beloved Uncle Timothy, who was thought to be as saintly a man that could ever be borne into a family.

At the time, in his early forties, he gave silent witness to the miracle at the sacrificial table. The wine had lost its natural viscosity and seemed thinner and bright like immediately oxidized blood pouring from a head wound. The bread had a moist, pasty appearance, nothing at all like the dry wafer stamped into a circle. It was jagged and malleable and, at first, frightened him into thinking he was hallucinating yet all the while knowing this was his life's work, his own passion meeting the Passion and suffering of our Lord. Countless hours, he had meditated on the Christ's divine sacrifice, barely comprehending, admittedly, the pain of derisive rejection only made greater by the intense physical injury upon injury. He looked up at his family members seated in the first five rows and cousins, third, fourth, and fifth generation. He glanced at the rich mahogany box with its waxed finish and draped with both an Irish and American flag and knew that God was revealing himself for a reason but not knowing why.

Uncle Tim was already a senior officer when he fought on the Italian front during the Second World War. He recalled the story told to him by his uncle, an amazing account of a documented event. As a bomber pilot, Uncle Tim was carrying out a mission to attack the city of San Giovanni Rotundi, birthplace of Padre Pio, the Capuchin priest now a popular mystic saint of the twentieth century. As the air squad dutifully set out to bomb the town, there appeared before them a brown-robed friar as a vision in the sky. All their efforts to unleash the bombs were fruitless. Only later, when Uncle Tim had entered the American base at Foggia (a nearby town) did he recognize the friar—on a chance encounter—as the one he had witnessed in the torrid sky above San Giovanni. Why he thought of his Uncle Tim and the Padre Pio story now perplexed him, especially since he posited the theory of an incarnate angel, not a human being experiencing episodes of bilocation.

He could debate further with his younger colleague but did not believe it would advance the case in either direction. He knew there was only one conclusive action to determine the how, what, where, and why of the story, if at all possible. He would arrange for the two to meet, Peggy and the present-day Lori.

17

In the Huddle

Peggy sat in a folding chair she dragged over from the corner of the spacious hall. It was midmorning, and she was performing community duties mandated by her school. At present, she was twenty hours behind in her total count. Mama Mitchell had arranged for a ten-hour service stint in the church hall through the New Year. Her job was to perform babysitting services while parishioners attended mass. She had one-half hour of silence and an empty venue before the next grouping of toddlers invaded her dutiful section. It was for the in-between time that she prearranged a meeting with the two priests, on her turf and her terms. The encounter would not be more than twenty-five minutes at the most, maybe twenty if a child was dropped off early, which often happened.

Peggy noticed the clergy through the glass partition upon entering the building adjacent to the church. She hunkered down in the middle of the room with her usual arm-folded stance and frowning face. Fathers Norton and O'Malley were in no way expecting a cheerful greeter but welcomed the opportunity to gather more evidence for their respective theories.

"Grab a chair," she yelled over as they entered the hall.

Neither anticipated much cooperation, but it was still worth every moment of learning more about the unnatural phenomenon.

"Good morning, Peggy. We appreciate your scheduling a meeting with us." Father Norton was all smiles and congeniality.

Resembling a stone-faced witness on the stand, she readied herself for the never-ending cross-examination. "So who's in charge here?"

"No one," said Father O'Malley, crossing an arthritic right knee and reclining as best he could in the hard-backed folding chair. In his youth, he took a spill from a motorcycle that nearly broke his shin bone and left gravel embedded in his kneecap. He still looked at that recuperative time as the onset of his vocation, time spent healing and completing an interior journey to his destined life.

Taking on a different posture, Father Norton leaned in like a quarterback in the huddle. "We're just as confused as you are, Peggy. We don't have any clear answers."

"Well, I certainly hope that's not why we're meeting 'cause I'm pretty sure I already knew that." Her snappy tongue belied her youthfulness. Never a believer in reincarnation, he still wondered how some young people had wizened personalities and some older people had seemingly eternal naiveté.

"Is she here now?" asked Father Norton.

Peggy burst into a giggle. "You really didn't ask that, did you? Why, Father if she were here, I would have pulled up a chair."

The young priest felt some ground slipping away, and Father O'Malley took the reins. "Peggy, I know Lori Hopkins. She's real and lives about fifty miles from here."

"One and the same?" Now Peggy got involved, leaning closer to the clergy, huddled in the winning football play.

Both Fathers were surprised at the split-second transformation. Here was a soul searching for an answer to anything in her life, but most especially, the mystery she was living out without a shred of understanding. Admittedly, their conjectures were not any further advanced, and the supernatural world was just as confounding to them as anyone lacking an education in deep theological perplexities.

"Okay, so now what? This is big. Don't you think? I mean really big. Wait, how do you know it's the same person?" Peggy's mind was reeling with the news, and nothing making sense finally made sense. She could throw her towel in the ring. No trying to figure this out. Plus, she had verbal ammunition to use against what she thought was a dead person coming back from the grave. Lori's alive! Lori's alive! Lori's alive! It was her instant mantra, her thread of truth, her link to sanity. "Wait 'til I see her," Peggy spoke under her breath, a slow grimace forming as the semblance of a smile.

"We still need to gather facts, Peggy, and the fact remains that she's appearing to you as a fourteen-year-old, stuck in a time machine of 1955." Father Norton made his usual attempt to gain ground. He wasn't by any stretch a pompous person, but he did have a legal mind and a courtroom approach to many situations. As a tribunal judge, in his second year, his canon law background imposed upon his approach to any given situation.

"Okay, so explain how she knew about Buddy Holly. He died in 1959."

"This supports my theory that she's bilocating." Father Norton welcomed the lead-in to posit his theory. "The spirit, specter, whatever you're experiencing, Peggy, is possibly the full grown, present-day Lori, but appearing as the one sixty years ago."

"But, my dear Father Norton," chimed in Father O'Malley, "that doesn't really make sense. Wouldn't she just appear as she would now, as a seventy-five-year-old woman?"

Father Norton readied himself to argue his point, only if to comprehend it more clearly himself! "Yes, in our world of logic. But time is really a continuum; and the past, present, and future are all here and now. Many times, Jesus appears with Our Lady as an infant."

"Yes, you speak of the divine, not human."

"Don't box in God, Father O'Malley."

Now Peggy was on the sidelines with a debate brewing. She rather enjoyed not being the only frustrated person in the mix even though she was desperate for answers. "Okay, I now have dueling priests, and this is getting me nowhere."

"May I suggest, once again, that an angel, possibly a guardian angel, is visiting you?" Father O'Malley rather enjoyed promoting his argument.

"You can make all the suggestions you want, Father. The truth won't be known until we visit the woman."

"Well, visiting Lori is a corporeal work of mercy at best since she does appear to be very much alone, but I don't see how it will solve our mystery." The old Irish priest waited for a response from his younger Germanic brother-in-Christ. He waited a minute or two as the opposing priest pondered what he said. Convinced that there would be no response, he continued. "Is this silent consent? We will just have to agree to disagree. Only God can solve an unearthly mystery. The key, Father, is really what we learn from this supernatural event. What is it that God wants us all to take away from it?"

Divided in her thoughts, Peggy, for just a few unbearable seconds, wished she had not met these two men of the cloth. Her reasoning made her uncomfortable. They were bringing God into the picture, and she'd spent most of her life avoiding thoughts of her Maker, the Supreme Being, and Creator of all living things. Evading God was never easy with a mother's devotion so palpable throughout the Mitchell household, in her mannerisms and incessant praying. Peggy felt tricked as if part of a ruse on her mom's prayer petitions for reparation. But Lori was real, and if not real, something she stumbled across that had swallowed her whole like Jonah living in the belly of the whale. Yes, she entered the pitch-dark cavity of the behemoth the day she unfalteringly entered Lori's trap. Indeed, she would see it through and meet the woman who was worn out by life and, she thought fleetingly, maybe that's what we really have in common. Young and worn out versus old and worn out. One, the big fish, the other waiting to be convulsed and eventually spat out onto a rocky shoreline and maybe, just maybe, a new life.

18

The Aftermath

Lori awaited Christmas with the greatest anticipation. She prided herself for bringing it back to life between the concrete walls of her father's safety box. She didn't believe that anything or anyone could survive a nuclear blast. Too many films, too many horror stories later, a sealed vault seemed fruitless. One week into her personally fashioned Christmas cave, she even thought about the Holy Family with no place to sleep driven out to a stable area only fit for grazing animals. A sense of comfort and peace warmed her within the cold, subterranean space. Random thoughts and deep slumber complemented her solitude. She experienced a renewed spirit, awaiting the birth of the Savior child.

* * *

The first on the scene was Lottie, stunned by the carnage. Tornado winds and severe storms hit three states. The housing cluster outside of Lubbock, Texas, or more accurately, three streets of a newly sprung neighborhood, were reduced to piles of sticks and bricks. The worst happened at 4:06 p.m., close to the twilight hour when her family of three would be readying for dinner. She imagined her daughter exhausted by Christmas preparations, preparing chicken and dumplings—a favorite of her husband's—totally unaware of death's proximity.

Remains of anyone—her daughter, son-in-law, and granddaughter—were yet to be found among the rubble so very soon after news arrived. She drove along a lonely highway in the longest hour of her life.

Walking along the endless debris, she stumbled across one of the exotic masks fully intact, no longer supported by the dining room wall. She always felt the guises hid unknown faces staring down with disdain at a table of plenty. A chill ran up Lottie's spine with thoughts of how minimal man's murderous wars were compared to the shock of Mother Nature's swift and sudden betrayal of everything in her path. Her mind wandered aimlessly through the catalog of similar memories, feeling detached from the present scene. In April 1935, she was in Lubbock, Texas, visiting a nurse friend. It was actually a Sunday, Black Sunday, on April 14.

For the south, especially in the Texas Panhandle, dirt, dust, and sandstorms were natural and unnatural occurrences. Even now, Lottie heard many refer to the decade as the "Dirty Thirties."

As an active mom and doctor's wife, Lottie had only traveled to the Lone Star state—or specifically Lubbock—on a few occasions, this visit marking her third to Lucille, an old school friend. Thanks to Fred, Lucille's Texan husband, she knew a bit of the history. The town was named after Colonel Thomas S. Lubbock, a Texas ranger. She also knew that the Panhandle comprised twenty-six of the northernmost counties in Texas. What she didn't know, from nearly a quarter century in Boston, was the inordinate suffering the South's denizens, people desperate for food, and an existence sans the fine soil that whipped through the air and coated their very lives.

The day, April 14, was pristine with blue skies, a marvel for the Dust Bowl inhabitants. Lottie's ears and sensibilities were jammed with horrific details of the previous month when five million acres of wheat were destroyed. Lottie mumbled, "Tsk tsk," shook her head several times, and attempted a look of exceptional pain, while Lucille prattled away with the fraught-filled news. Not witnessing any of these events herself, Lottie mustered all her inner resolve not to become the Doubting Thomas. After three days, she was euphoric about her return to New England. If the air was slightly unbreathable due to residual sand grains, it was further constricted with Lucille's tales of woe, oftentimes about uprooted families that Lottie had never met.

On that particular Sunday morning, Lottie rose to a resplendent, clear vista and a brilliantly blue horizon. She remained in awe of such wide-open space, a premium in her crowded urban surroundings at home.

After an early dinner of rabbit stew of which she choked down, Lottie hugged Lucille one last time while surreptitiously checking her watch and awaiting Fred to back out his pickup truck from the barn. Standing on the porch, she noticed way out on the horizon what looked like a wall of foggy, ominous clouds.

"Look, a storm is heading our way. I better get to the train station soon before it hits."

Lucille, facing the front door, slowly turned her head. "That's no regular storm, and they ain't no rain clouds, Lottie. They ain't clouds." In a deadpan tone of surrender, she continued, "It's the dust. Dear Lord, I've never seen anything like it. Never." Her next breath, a shrill siren, echoed in the eerie silence. "Fred, get out of the barn. Look what's comin'!"

Fred drove out of the barn and immediately reversed his truck, jumped out, and slammed the barn door shut. Yelling and running, "Git in the house!" he shoved both women in the front door.

"That's dust?" said Lottie, years later convinced it was the most naïve and slightly arrogant statement of the century.

Standing in the parlor, windows and shutters closed, the house growing darker than the darkest hour before dawn, sand pelting the roof, wind whistling and howling, and the screeching of birds with useless wings, Lucille held her friend's hand and pumped it with a kind, reassuring warmth.

"If we were out there for one more minute, we might all be blind by now. Those grains of sand hit like a spray of bullets."

Lottie looked at her friend's silhouette in total wonder at her calm bravery and never doubted her again. From that day forward, whenever Lucille called to chat, she gave her undivided and loving attention.

* * *

Black and white police cars, swirling red-shaded streams of light, approached from a distance. Five leveled ranch houses created a gaping, shocking reminder of loss. Lottie Mitchell was stunned by the aura of peace in her soul. Maybe it was really shock masquerading as serene submission. She wasn't quite sure. Maybe it was witnessing with compassionate eyes the many tragedies of war at an early age. No long pain-filled suffering this time. Her daughter was her lifeblood, her only connection to her beloved soul mate. An undeniable serenity coursed through every vein like some strong, heavenly elixir. Police cars and ambulances with screeching sirens lined up, a barricade against the devastation. A lanky reporter from the local newspaper walked slowly toward her. She braced herself for a moment that would snap her back to harsh and bitter reality.

"Are you a neighbor?" said the young man with a brown fedora and tan overcoat. Pen poised for remarks, he smiled only to warm up the potential interviewee.

And the earth turned, tilted, and twisted, leaving a cold slap of sheer misery enfolding Lottie, wrapping its icy, stinging claws around her broken heart. A quick shiver, a wave of nausea, and then a direct question barely whispered. "Why are you smiling?"

"I'm sorry," said the cub reporter, pushing his hat back, revealing a shiny forehead and slightly furrowed brow. "Was this your family?"

Lottie succumbed to deep sorrow and confided in the stranger searching for morsels of a story. "Yes, it's my family, my daughter, her husband, and…" she could not bear to say the word.

The reporter waited a few seconds and asked, "Yes, and anyone else?"

"My daughter. Her name is Mir, Miriam. My son-in-law is Tom…Tom Hopkins." Lottie fixated on the young man's brown oxfords, anything but eye the rubble, the broken bits of household items strewn carelessly across the immediate horizon.

The reporter waited for more story. "No one else?" Lottie was lost in thoughts of her precious Lori.

Mere moments later, a highway police officer strolled up to take control of the situation. He tipped his hat and spoke in the somber tone and manner of someone attending a wake. "Ma'am, we'll take over for now. We just have a few questions and would like to verify some information with you."

The reporter hung back, hungry for more information, while the police officer blocked him from further discourse. "I think you'll have to wait for your story."

"Could I get your name, please, to follow up on?" He needed a story right now to take back to the newsroom and was hoping someone in town knew the family.

"Charlotte Mitchell," she replied, emotionless as if a guilty party in an investigation. She felt another wave of agonizing grief and wished she had been there with the family, swept away by the fierce, deadly whip of winds that descended on her beloved daughter and granddaughter's household. She tilted her head and glanced over at the gleaming eye of the Raggedy Ann doll she had clutched only a few days ago in the cozy comfort of Lori's bedroom sanctuary.

Lori, the light of her life, somewhere among the carnage. Five families were missing, that was the last count. The newsman, without a story, shrugged his bony shoulders and sauntered back to a slightly unstylish 1950 Buick with brackets of grillwork resembling miniature prison bars. He started the engine only to hear another motor like that of a purring cat. The sultry yet lilting voice of Eartha Kitt spilled out softly across the airwaves into the wasteland and wreckage. "Santa baby, slip a sable under the tree, for me. I've been an awful good girl Santa Baby, and hurry down the chimney tonight."

Lottie listened intently, sifting through recent recollections, her mind clearing away the shock waves. Tears streamed down her face. The police officer offered a gentle hand to her shoulder. Miss Kitt warbled in her coquettish manner: "Santa Baby, an out-of-space convertible too, light blue I'll wait up for you dear, Santa baby, and hurry down the chimney tonight."

"My granddaughter Lori. She's underground." Tears streamed, a flood of tears. Tears of gladness, tears of trust in knowing the truth, paying attention to the signs. Lori asked for the song before Christmas so she could play it while entertaining her friends in her hideaway. Every hope sprung forth from Lottie's heart. The reporter, seeing the frantic woman run to a spot of earth, and fall to the ground, shut off the car engine and returned to the scene. He had a story, more than he ever imagined.

A loud, persistent knocking on the cellar door awoke Lori before the beam of a flashlight spilled across the steps. Blinking furiously, she covered her head with the softly knitted angora throw that seasonally draped her bed.

"Lori," bellowed her grandmother as she descended the stairs. She poked her head out from under her makeshift tent, immediately alarmed by Lottie's wild gestures and frozen gaze. "Thank God, thank God, my Lori, thank God." She wiped away streams of tears from her half-smiling face, an odd mix of joy and sorrow.

"What's wrong, Grandma? Why are you crying?" Lori absentmindedly pulled the throw close to her chest, unknowingly bracing herself for unthinkable and unutterable news.

Lottie fell to her knees at Lori's feet. Three police officers with flashlights peered at every square inch of the cheerfully decorated bomb shelter in sheer amazement at the Christmas spectacle. "I was so afraid I lost you." Lottie's sobbing was fully unleashed. "Everything, everyone is gone. And I thought you were too. But you're safe."

"Mrs. Mitchell, maybe we should get you and your granddaughter above ground." The police officer held out a hand to help her back up. Lottie remained fixed at Lori's feet, words escaping her. Nothing she'd ever experienced, no words to families of their dead sons from the ravages of war could compare to what she would soon confide to her daughter's only child.

Lottie studied the puzzled face with its lovely turned up nose and light spray of freckles. "There's nothing I can say to prepare you, dear." She dug deep into her nursing background, back to a time when she was the bearer of bad news, knowing full well that speaking in plain, simple, and straightforward words was the most effective manner of dealing with sudden loss. "A tornado touched down a little over an hour ago, right here. It took everything and everyone in its path, Lori. There are no survivors on this street. Five houses, five families. I'm sorry, sweetheart. I'm so very sorry. We'll get through this. I just need to let you know that there's no house, no signs of life. Everything is gone."

Lori searched her Grandma's face for some hope that none of what she heard was true. *How could it be? It must be a dream, a horrible, bad dream*, she thought, *and I'll awake, and everything will be okay*. As Lori emerged slowly from her safety, a sudden hatred for Christmas and all things joyful crept into her heart, imprisoning it with unrelenting claws. The Grinch was no competition for Lori's love turned inside out to hate. The poor, unsuspecting Grinch never knew what love had waiting for him. His cold heart grew three sizes larger, while Lori's large heart shrunk, hardening into a stony, unfeeling, unemotional semblance. Yes, it pumped the blood through her veins, actually in a throbbing, temple-bursting, unnatural manner that made her dizzy with its palpitations. But the heart of hearts, the very center of her soul had frozen as she experienced the first taste of bitterness.

"Lori." Lottie knew that her granddaughter was experiencing emotional shock. She also knew the best remedy, to remove the victim from the scene. "Let's go, sweetheart." She cradled the devastated young lady in a protective embrace. "There's nothing here for us for now. We can come back later. Let the police and rescue team do their work. There's nothing we can do right now."

"No. I want to stay and help with the rescue." Lori dug her feet into the littered ground, knelt down, and clawed at the earth.

A rescue team member approached them. Behind him, the cub reporter aimed his camera, capturing a serene look of jubilation from the family guardian and distorted lines of anguish from the young survivor. Lori turned away and wiped the dirt in her hands across her blank face.

19

Peg O' My Heart

Peggy and Lori eked out a comfortable life together. They knew very little about each other, only that unpredictable moments were the course of their adventure. Every now and then, Peggy would awake, thinking she dreamt up the whole ordeal, only to be reminded by Fran and Larry that, *yes*, they all entered the preserved bomb shelter, and, *no*, neither of her accomplices have encountered an extraterrestrial being, ghost, or any manifestation resembling the all too accurate description of Lori, practically counting the freckles on the bridge of her nose.

Fran, the interrogator, dragged Peggy to the school library after delving into the town records. Calling up the digitized archives, he noted a massively destructive tornado that touched down in Lubbock on Sunday, December 18, one week before Christmas, which fell on the following Sunday in the year 1955.

"From what it looks like, your friend's house was totally obliterated," said Fran, sounding like a crime investigator.

"Okay, so first, she's not my friend…well, not really, and second, so what? How does it help me?"

Fran studied her reed-thin frame, nearly similar to his own. The androgynous twins, he chuckled to himself. Angular bones jutting out at elbows and knees yet with a visage seductively plain and eyes alternating joy and sorrow between each blink. He was trying to understand her plight, trying to put himself in her shoes, the altruistic route. Her wooden Indian statue stance, guarding the front of cigar shops, was becoming all too familiar these days. The whole scenario sounded too unreal and irrational, but he liked Peggy and wanted desperately to bring her comfort.

"I don't know, Peg O' My Heart."

"Stop it. Don't make fun of me."

"I would never make fun of you, Peg…Peggy." Skipping a beat, he gripped a chair, twirled it around, and leaned forward against its back. "We've known each other since third grade. I'll never forget that day when you stole my recess milk. I thought, there's the girl of my dreams."

"You're doing it again. Stop making fun. I'm really hurting, and no one cares or understands." The "poor me" pout made her unadorned features even more alluring.

"Don't do that because I melt or just cave in, and I have something really important to tell you." He searched her face for a reaction.

"Don't tell me. You're moving, right?" Peggy had a deep dread of abandonment contradicting her other deep desire for solitude.

"No, I'm not leaving town. I'm leaving my past behind. No more heists. I'm through. If I could return all the stuff I've lifted, pocketed, or stolen in the last few years, I'd do it in a heartbeat. But I'm not going to beat myself up anymore. It's done, it's over. I can't change my past. To be honest, I'm not even sure I'd want to change anything." They sat quietly, letting the truth seep into the silence.

"The question is, why did you do it in the first place?"

Peggy wanted the answer for herself really. She didn't understand half of her own motives although sometimes recognized a veil of anger over her emotions, one that rarely lifted for a clearer vision of her immediate circumstances at any given time.

"Who knows? Maybe to see what I could get away with since that's what I've been doing most of my life. Cheating. Now the cheater feels cheated."

Peggy felt an irrepressible smile curling her lips. "Larry will probably beat the crap out of you, like the carcasses in his dad's freezer."

Now they were both laughing. They laughed until they bent over, clutching their midsections and eventually rolling from side to side on the moss green and brown-speckled carpet as if it was a pile of crispy autumn leaves. The school librarian, Mrs. Hitchens, startled them with her navy Croc shoes and sturdy legs spread slightly in an imposing stance.

Fran bolted up with a ready response. "I lost my pen, Mrs. Hitchens. Here it is!"

Frowning her best, the maven of books held her ground like a sentinel. As a retired elementary schoolteacher, she volunteered in the junior high library to escape the drudgery of life in an empty house since the death of Mr. Hitchens, a retired high school teacher, three months earlier. "I don't think I need to remind you that this is a library, and there's no talking," she whispered as if telling a confidence.

Peggy whispered back, "We weren't talking."

"I know you were laughing and carrying on, and any loud noise is prohibited. Now if you continue, I'll have to ask you to leave. No loud noise, no talking, no cell phones." Mrs. Hitchens pointed to the card tent that spelled out her litany of rules.

"We were just getting ready to leave anyway, Mrs. Hitchens. Thanks and have a nice day." Fran made a gesture to Peggy, and they headed for the exit.

"You always suck up to people. I don't get it." Peggy drew up her coat collar. Even a slight chill found its way to her bones, and the gray sky offered no beams of warmth. "Will we see you?" She inspected her bare hands and opened a palm, searching for a lifeline pointed out to her by Matilda who studied signs and symbols.

"I said I'm not going anywhere. Sure, I'll be around. We can catch a movie or something." Fran shoved his hands in his pockets, a comfortable, familiar gesture when he was searching for the right words and could not find even one.

"Okay, well, I'll see you around, then. Are you going to tell Larry? We still have some stuff, inventory I guess. What do you want to do with it?"

Peggy cared even less than Fran about the pilfered items. She was more eager than him to end the looting escapades but was too preoccupied by life and Lori to set a course of action. Father O'Malley had gotten to her with his patience and nonjudging ways. Although not ready to come completely clean like the Psalm he read to her, "Create in me a clean heart," she recognized her disordered spirit and how much misery she had brought on herself. And here, for so many years, she thought misery was placed upon her by others. From her earliest memories, she blamed a houseful of siblings and a mother stretched beyond human capacity to properly care for her brood.

"Charity begins at home," her mom would say, yet she witnessed nothing but uncharitable acts between brothers and sisters, father and mother, and even the cat and dog who circled each other warily. Before Fran and Peggy parted ways, she sized him up and thought maybe the visits with the priests had a similar effect on him, an inadvertent path to soul searching.

"Fran, have you been to confession?" It sounded almost accusatory, like a betrayal of their unlawful theft.

"No, but I'm thinking about it. Hey, one thing at a time. Why do you ask?" Fran rarely entertained probing questions. His distance was calculated, and Peggy thought she'd never know what he was really thinking. He seemed a stranger to himself more than anyone else.

"Just wondering. Okay, I have an idea, but I'm not sure it will work." Thoughts tumbled through Peggy's head. She needed to rid herself of stolen items translated into deprivation of peace and, ultimately, joy. She thought about the little purloined prince coveted by her youngest sibling. How did Lori miss that stealthy act? Or maybe she didn't, and maybe she wanted Peggy to nab it all along.

"Okay so what are you conniving now?" Fran was already removed by a few game spaces. He'd already received his free "Do Not Go to Jail" card, and he knew it. He was bailing out and not owning up to any of his past sins, at least not publicly.

"So I'm holding the bag, right?" Peggy penetrated his chest with her stare, daring not to look angrily into his eyes for fear that the anger would melt, and the tears would flow. "What about the money we split up?" Now she would start an examination. It just seemed like the natural progression following a swift and unpredictable turning point.

"Oh, I'll find some use for it, even if I donate it to charity." Fran wasn't ready to delve into the particulars of his past transgressions, and it became more obvious.

"How noble of you." Peggy could feel the sarcasm dripping from her words, and it was only the beginning. There was no honor among thieves, no honor in any sin, and she felt stripped and bare, awaiting the stoning from other sinners.

"I'm not expecting any absolution from you." Fran was ready to stand his ground. He felt no intimidation, no wavering from his new course.

"It's one step a time. I don't know what I'll do, I only know what I won't do, and that's a start."

Now he felt sorry for Peggy because he sensed viscerally that she felt abandoned, a reaction he was not anticipating but now realized he should have expected. "I'll see you in school, Monday."

Hands shoved back in pockets signaled the end of the conversation, the end of explanations, maybe the end of a friendship, even if forged in a "thick as thieves" fashion. Stepping away, he suddenly turned back. "Wait, you didn't tell me your plan."

"That's because I don't know it yet."

Fran nodded slowly and walked away, immediately feeling a hole in his heart growing bigger and filling with the mercy of God. Peggy watched, her own aching heart awaiting some small triumph.

The following day, Lori practically ambushed her from behind, startling an immensely preoccupied Peggy. "Don't you ever knock?" she muttered while picking up her scattered belongings.

"When are you going to invite me to your house?" Lori retorted.

"Oh, don't act so innocent. You've been to my house and scared the living crap out of my punky sister."

"Yes, but you never invited me!"

"You need an invite? You come and go in my life as you please, and now you want an engraved invitation? I don't get you at all!" Peggy reached in her jacket for her iPhone.

"Well, you don't have to get mad at me. I'm just trying to be a friend."

Peggy dropped to her knees and assumed a cross-legged position in the grass along the sidewalk.

"What are you doing?" Lori said, hovering above her.

"Having a nervous breakdown. Want to join me?" She texted Larry about the Fran news. "I'm knee-deep in crap I don't want, and I can't find my way out." She searched her shoulder bag. "Where's a joint when you need one?"

Lori plopped down next to her. "Maybe I can help."

Peggy shook her head and stared at the ground. "Where do I start?" She threw her head back for her version of a silent scream, rounding out her mouth and not emitting any sound.

"Okay, I have five dozen iPhone cases. They're worth ninety-eight dollars retail, and I can sell them for twenty-five a pop, and that's about five hundred for each of the three partners. And that's only the beginning. I have cameras, about two hundred, that sell for ninety bucks in stores, and I can sell them for fifty each, so that's another ten grand. Should I continue?"

"How did you get all of these items?" Lori asked innocently.

Peggy went for the jugular. "The same way you got your precious box of buttons."

"Oh, so you stole them," replied Lori with unexpected insouciance. "And you want to give them back. Is that right?"

"It's too late. I can't give them back. It's stolen property." Peggy tore up pieces of grass and threw the blades onto the path in front of her.

"Well, you don't have to sell them. That just compounds the act of stealing, right?"

Peggy was agitated and wished she had not broached the topic. "Stop asking me these questions. You're no help at all."

"You don't want these things, so get rid of them. You have a moral obligation to return the items to their owner."

"But they don't have an owner." Peggy buried her face between her knees.

"Yes, they do. Someone owned them. Just return them."

"I'll go to jail. Do you want to visit me behind bars? You might be the only one!"

"Geez, I didn't say hand-deliver them! Oh, and you also have to make atonement."

"What?" Peggy felt dizzy. She didn't want to talk about the stolen property weighing her down, especially any notion of returning to the crime scene.

"Just return it. You'll find a way."

A new text message buzzed across her screen. Larry was creative with his expletives and basically said there would be hell to pay. "Hey, I have an idea." Peggy tapped her camera icon and pointed the phone at Lori. "Say cheese." She tapped again, capturing a surprised and startled Lori. Peering into the screen, she saw proof of nothing, only the ground below, the sky above, and the wide-open space of unspent dreams. She rose to her feet and gathered her belongings. The silky, white feather, left unnoticed, curled its way through the air and down the path behind her as she made her way home.

Larry was waiting at the Stop sign two blocks from her house, knowing her familiar route. He paced back and forth, chewing vigorously on a popsicle stick. He waved at her with both arms, just in case she didn't notice him, which made her chuckle. Larry was a ticking time bomb. She figured he'd live for maybe another twenty years, if he was lucky.

"So Mr. A.H. himself called it quits, huh? Well, I got news for both of you, and I was going to tell you later today. Everything's sold, all of it. Every frickin' thing in our inventory, S-O-L-D. Gone forever. I have the cash here, but I'm not splittin' it three ways, only 'tween you and me. Mr. Sorry Sack won't mind, going clean and all. It's fifteen grand, so that's seven and a half Gs for you and the rest for me."

"Who bought it?" Peggy heard every word like an echo from a conch shell with waves crashing on a distant seashore. The heaviest of burdens was lifted, and she felt almost weightless as if floating two inches, no two feet off the ground.

"Some street vendor dude from New York. Can you believe it? I undersold a bit so he'd make his profit margin. What a racket, huh?" Larry handed her a large brown envelope stuffed with one hundred dollar bills. "Here's seventy Benjamins, I still owe you."

Peggy hugged the envelope to her chest. "Larry, you are an angel of mercy. Unwittingly, but *yes* an angel of mercy." Stretching out her arms, she presented the package back to him as if bearing a gift. "I want you to donate my take. You must donate it. I don't even want to see it. Just give it to your favorite charity."

Larry snatched the envelope with utter disbelief. "What are you doing waving this around like it's junk mail. Are you freakin' crazy?" Taking a breath to calm down, he softened his tone. "I don't have a favorite charity. I am my own favorite charity. What are you saying?"

Peggy took him by both shoulders and gave him one of those square-in-the-face looks. "Larry, it's a grace. A total grace. Please give it to a local charity. Anonymously."

"You're nuts, both you and Fran the freak." He paced and chewed for a full minute, finally spitting out orange-flavored splinters. "Okay, I'll give it to an animal shelter. Is that okay with you, Madame Do Good?" Inside, Larry was doing a full-blown handspring. His heart—in some small, charity-filled corner—expanded a centimeter or two at the thought of giving comfort and food to lost and abandoned cats and dogs. "You're sure?" Larry waved the envelope under her nose as if it held the aroma of freshly baked bread.

"Larry, you don't know the half of it. Just trust me, I'm good with this one." Peggy checked her iPhone. "I've got to haul my butt home, or Mother Mary will be sending out a search party. Just make sure that money goes to a charity, okay?"

"Yes, Mother Teresa, I heard you the first time."

Peggy smirked and Larry gave his best shrug. "What can I say? I can't do this on my own. You're both making me look bad."

"No one's making you look bad. Let's not do the blame game thing, okay? We're all guilty, and we know it. No excuses. I've really got to go." Without warning, Peggy hugged Larry surprising herself even more than him.

"Okay, all right already, that's enough." Larry was nearly crimson with embarrassment. He stared down, trying to regain his composure. "What's this, you moltin' or something?" Larry bent over and picked up the slim, oily white feather lying at his toe tip.

Peggy held it up to the failing light of day. "Well, what do you know? Her true colors."

"True colors?" Larry looked confused.

"More like true nature." She slipped the feather in her pocket and turned the corner too filled with emotion to look back. She signaled her final wave from behind and disappeared, out of sight. Larry banged his head into the Stop sign post and tucked the envelope in his jacket, its weighty contents dragging him down to an imaginary netherworld.

20

Cross My Heart

Lori spent her first two weeks of the New Year 1956 out of school and out of commission. She kept to herself, not seeing any of her friends. Grandma Mitchell rarely left her side, sharing a room and, at times, the same bed. Lori missed the Christmas concert and the school dance featuring the up-and-coming Elvis. Christmas was no more than another day of grieving, and Lottie did not want to force any festivities upon her brokenhearted granddaughter. The Christmas room, not entered since she emerged that fateful day, was abandoned. The entire state of Texas, the entire universe could be left to oblivion as far as Lori was concerned. Lottie exercised patience with her beloved little one, now a teenager. She could relate to the young lady growing quickly into womanhood yet clinging to the innocent, unencumbered ways of childhood. Lori returned to school on a particularly mild and sunny Monday morning. Her grandmother, now her guardian, kissed her on the cheek and studied the fragile young lady's profile.

"I don't want to go back to school," confided Lori. "I can't face any of my friends. I just want to move somewhere else. What about Boston? Can we go to Boston?"

Grandma Lottie understood grief all too well. She rarely, if ever, considered reminding Lori that she had lost her only child and a cherished son-in-law who devoted his time to making a happy home. "It's too cold in the winter," her guardian shrugged.

Lori gave her grandma a blank stare that sent a tiny chill through her body. "I like the cold. I prefer the cold." Lori wasn't ready to give in. She knew her way around Grandma Lottie. She knew how to wear her down with little, if any, persistence.

Grandma waved her hand as if it held a magic wand. How many times had she chastised her daughter for such an expression of dismissal? And she was the propagator. She caught herself and placed both hands on the steering wheel. Reaching over, she gave Lori a quick peck on the cheek in every attempt to lighten the gravity, the heaviness, and the potential joylessness in their personal worlds. "You'll be late, Pumpkin."

Lori turned her head away and fixed her gaze on the awaiting school and all of its familiarity now seeming so distant. "Don't call me that. My dad did, and I never want to hear it ever again." Lori wiped away the tear tracing down her cheek. She faced Lottie.

"I'm sorry, sweetheart. Let's just get through this school year, okay? We'll go to Boston in the summer. For a visit."

Clutching the car door handle, she paused and turned to her grandma. "Promise?"

Lottie searched Lori's eyes for any glimmer of joy. Her smile was the saddest she'd ever seen. Pulling her close, she hugged her tightly and stroked her strawberry blonde hair caught up in a ponytail. "Cross my heart."

21

Mental Notes

Peggy played out the role of a Dutch uncle or, in this case, a Dutch aunt. She assumed Lori wasn't going anywhere anytime soon and wouldn't divulge the reason for her manifestation. Three weeks into their relationship, Christmas was nearing, and Peggy felt inclined to blurt out the details of Lori's family tragedy. Hopefully, it would trigger some new phase of their relationship or, even better, end it abruptly. Just possibly, speaking the truth about the facts would put Lori back in the time she belonged, wherever and whenever that was in the continuum of past, present, and future. Lori sat on their park bench, the one that illuminated their *I Love Lucy* connection, and waited for her freckled and fickle alter ego. She kicked her legs and recalled the first meeting with the eerie figure seemingly born out of thin air stretching a hand through the lines of time for her box of buttons. The haunting image sent a new shiver through her slender corpus, and she clasped her arms around her petite bosom.

"Boo!" shouted Lori from behind Peggy, erupting her silent reflections.

"What the—" howled a startled Peggy, whipping her head around to see a gloating Lori standing arms folded and grinning like a genie that just escaped from a century-old stay in its bottle.

"Got ya, huh?" Lori said as she climbed over the bench and sat next to a grumbling, mumbling, and slightly perturbed subject of her prank.

"You're already a ghost. Why do you have to act like one? Isn't that like overkill?" Peggy rubbed her ear not so much because it hurt, but for the sheer impertinence of Lori's actions. She detested practical jokes and never, ever considered the words practical and joke to have an association. "I need to fill you in on what happened on December 18, 1955. I'm thinking you must have fallen asleep or something in your little lair, and the whole neighborhood or most of it was destroyed." Peggy waited for a response, wondering if she was digging too deep into a tragedy.

"Well, I think we already established that part. There's nothing left, and it's now, what year is it again?"

"It's 2015, sixty years later. Okay, so you don't need to hear all the details." Peggy resorted to inspecting her nails as they sat wordlessly, and with added poignancy, at a loss for words. After about five minutes, Peggy pierced the silence. "I remember a bad storm about four years ago when I was ten. It was a dust storm. They called it a Haboob or something."

Lori giggled. "A what? A Haboob?"

Peggy replied indignantly, "There really isn't anything funny about it, so I don't know why you're cackling. Anyway, it was October 17, and the winds were like seventy-five miles per hour. Trees came down, power lines, wildfires. It looked like the end of the world around here."

"My world ended sixty years ago." Lori twirled her fingers, head drooping, her voice low and sad.

Peggy continued her recount, "Everything stopped. The sky turned like a deep orange, all dust, and you couldn't see the hand in front of you. It was crazy. The news people said the dust cloud was eight thousand feet high as it moved through Lubbock."

Lori perked up. "Sounds like a story my Grandma Lottie told me about back in the 1930s, the Dust Bowl caused by a drought. When you have all that dry weather, it doesn't take much of a wind to carry the dust around."

Peggy steered the course back to her story. "Well, the storm I'm talking about really hit the state of Tennessee and ripped at least twenty homes from their foundations."

"Anyone dead?" Lori interrupted again.

"No, just dozens of people hurt," Peggy replied.

"Why are you telling me then?" Lori looked at her quizzically.

"I guess you reminded me of a strange story I recall from the storm. A little girl—I think three years old, blonde, and blue-eyed—was found in a field in Indiana, carried by the storm. I don't know how far away her family was, but they did identify her." Peggy leaned forward. "Sometimes, you remind me of someone who was blown into my life from some storm in the past, like that little girl found in a field far away from her home."

Unfazed, Lori, changed the course of their dialogue. "I made some mental notes, some words I don't understand. I'm hoping you can help me."

Peggy rolled her eyes in exasperation. "Go ahead."

"Okay, iPad. Does that have anything to do with feminine hygiene?" Lori knitted her eyebrows with so much concern that Peggy burst into a fit of laughing.

"You mean the rag? Are you kidding?" She admitted to herself that, many times, Lori was a source of utter entertainment, a constant reminder of how much the world had changed in such a short period of time. Even her own mother recalled a period without smartphones or flat screen computers and televisions. She reached into her jacket pocket. "Look, this is an iPod. I download, I mean, I guess in your day, more like record music. It records music."

"Did you steal that little gadget? Is it like a transistor radio? I asked for one for Christmas. They're all the rage!"

"You're changing the topic, and no, I did not steal it. I bought it. An iPad can be a camera, a phone, an electronic notebook, a computer."

"Oh, that's the other word. What did you call it? Computer?"

"Easy one. It's an electronic brain. It stores memory, like a brain. They had them back in your day, you know." Peggy barely tolerated being quizzed, and her short fuse was finally lit.

"Don't you get tired of it all?" Lori remarked nonchalantly.

"I wouldn't talk, you have a freakin' TV in your hideaway. What's that all about?"

Lori nodded. "You got me on that one. Okay, just one more. Can you take me to a church?"

Peggy screwed up her face. "Why?"

"It's where I'll find Christmas again. I think it will take me where I need to go."

Peggy kept quiet. She had no retort. Anything was worth trying if it relieved her of the burden of her private visitation. "I'll take you there tomorrow."

"What day would that be?" Lori was more direct than ever.

"Saturday."

"No, Sunday. Take me there Sunday."

Lori was winning this one, suspected Peggy as she wondered what would happen if she refused. Then again, a refusal would solve nothing. "Why?" asked Peggy in a confrontational tone.

"Why not?" Lori quipped with a smile. "It's a date then. Add it to your little computer, in case you forget."

"Oh, I won't forget," muttered Peggy as she envisioned an expression of utter delight on her mom's face as she accompanied her to church.

Walking home in solitude, Peggy noticed her father's green Chevy van parked in the driveway. Her heart sunk into a bottomless dry well.

22

The Lion's Den

Jack Mitchell, at forty-five, resembled a burly lumberjack with plaid flannel jacket, craggy features, and ruddy complexion supported by a chiseled, dimpled chin. Most days, he looked about ten years older than he was, especially after a day or two bender. On his random week days and nights home, all moods shifted from modest merriment to blatant cringing.

Mary Mitchell transformed from a placid, peaceful matriarch to a gazelle in the wilds of Africa all too wary of a hungry lion crouching down and ready to pounce. Running would only begin the chase and eventually lead to her being devoured. No, the best defense was to remain still and aware. If the pounce took place, she would then try her best to leap to safety. And all of these attacks were of a verbal nature for Jack had a vicious tongue when imbibing. His unarticulated fears surfaced with vitriolic words to any nearby target. Mary made sure she was the easiest mark to spare their children the insults and abusive comments. Most of them remained oblivious to his odious presence, for it seemed the best defense. They all had experienced the sting of his sarcasm and belittling, and somehow developed a protective layer fostered by the counterbalance of a saintly mother whose prayer petitions called upon constant protection from her patron, the mother of God.

Mary remembered a time when her life partner was more carefree and calm of spirit. They met in high school. Jack was the star quarterback and bore a resplendent smile with pearly white teeth complementing a beautifully chiseled chin. *Dashing* is the word that best described him. Mary was the president of the school library and found more company in the pages of books than in the noisy space of homeroom or lunchtime in the cafeteria. They were the quintessential opposites who attract.

Peggy braced herself. The entranceway smelled of a generic hotel body and face lotion, a blend of lilies, or some other exotic flower with an aromatic base. She thought her dad must use an entire complimentary bottle before arriving home. Maybe there was a part of him that enjoyed the anticipation of being united with his family. She learned to dread the hint of these blossoms that filled her nostrils. It was so contradictory to what he was all about, and she loathed, loved, and pitied him all at once for she wholeheartedly believed he had no way out of his alcoholism. The mere scent of the hastily applied floral creams evoked that much emotion. Making her way through the living room area, she was greeted by a broad smile from her dad reclining peacefully in his green fake leather recliner. He clearly had not had a drink. Not yet. It was only a mere matter of time, hours, or even minutes. Something, anything would set him off and give him an excuse to quench the awaiting demon.

"Where've you been?" he said with a surly tone that diminished any semblance of cheeriness.

"Library," answered Peggy as she glided through the room, avoiding eye contact and hoping a one-word answer would disengage and diffuse any mounting attempts at conversation.

"Doing what?" He now had a target for his growing irritation. "Don't walk away, I'm asking you a question."

Peggy stood in the middle of the room. Four pairs of sibling eyes were on her, peering out of noiseless, emotionless masks for faces. Michael, Martin and Martha—whom she nicknamed Marty One and Marty Two—and Miriam appeared like eerie child-sized mannequins in a storefront window. Peggy executed her best eye roll while jutting out a bony hip and folding sinewy arms.

"Research, Dad, okay?"

"What are you researching?"

Peggy believed he didn't bother to feign interest as he occupied himself before making his way to the liquor store, unless he'd already done so, and was painfully biding his time.

"Aren't you going to sit with us? Tell me what you're researching."

"Tornadoes. I'm really tired." She moved through the room and tripped over a stray boot.

"Are you hungry, dear?" her mother's angelic voice rang through the air, the ultimate peacemaker and matron for her brood.

"Just tired. I'll see ya'll in the morning." She yawned to punctuate her point.

"Well, I won't be here in the morning. I have another two-week road trip starting bright and early." Jack eased his arms over his head and clasped his hands together.

Aha, thought Peggy, *so that's why he's not skunked.* "Okay, well, see you when you get back. I'm really shot in the ass."

A somewhat horrified Mary reacted quickly, "Peggy, mind your manners and your tongue, please!"

"Okay, like I said, I'm really tired. I just need rest before I fall over. Good night, everyone." She made another move, and her relentless father continued.

"Your mom says you're flunking out of school," he continued with a perceived feeble attempt at parental concern.

"Can we discuss this some other time?" Now Peggy was annoyed and feeling trapped. Very close to walking out the front door, she projected her escape.

"Jack, it's okay. I can see Peggy's not feeling well. Nothing will change overnight, so let's just let her be for now."

Peggy looked at her mom's vapid eyes and innocuous smile. *She's worn-out more than I am*, she thought.

Keeping her sober husband company was a drain, like the babysitting gig that goes three hours overtime, and you just want out. The grandfather clock chimed eight, and no one spoke a word. All those watchful, silent eyes. It was too bizarre, and Peggy began putting one foot in front of the other while the clock rang out. She stepped in time with it, until she reached the hallway.

"Good night, everyone," she halfway whispered back, hoping for no command to return to the family scene resembling an odd bowl of still life.

"Pleasant dreams, dear," her mother replied.

Silent accord from her father sparked a tumble of thoughts from his seventh offspring. He was probably wondering how in God's world he was going to stay sober over the next few hours. He needed someone to torture, if not himself. Maybe he'll just fall asleep and be gone in a few hours.

Once in her room, Peggy kept the ceiling light off, creeping along the floor in search of her bed. With the door closed behind her, the pitch-black effect was overwhelmingly consoling. Feeling its outline, she plunged in as if jumping off a swinging tree branch into a summertime watering hole.

"*Ouch!*" yelled the victim of Peggy's funny bone smack in the jugular.

"What the hell's wrong with you? Lori is that you? What are you doing here?" Peggy jolted up.

"Lori? Who's Lori?" The warm figure reached for the bedside lamp in one quick motion.

Peggy blinked furiously as light brought clarity to her intruder's identity who resumed the barrage.

"Well, I've heard of Goldilocks, but I'm far from her, and this ain't no fairy tale. Your bed was my chosen retreat, so deal with it, spaghetti arms. And tell me, who the hell is Lori? Oh wait, let me guess. You're a lesbian. I should've known. All that serious attitude as a kid. Not that being serious is a bad thing, but on you, it was like a black cloud…"

"Enough already!" uttered Peggy, slicing through the ad nauseam commentary. "I thought you were in the jungle! What are you doing back in Texas?"

"I'll answer that if you tell me who Lori is."

"I'm not gay or bisexual or…look it's nothing, and you wouldn't believe it anyway, so tell me why you're here!"

"Peru was a total bust. I mean, it rained and rained, and when it didn't rain, it was wet. I felt soggy, everything was soggy. I just wanted to be dry. I actually started missing the tumbleweeds, the parched air, and the dry throat that was quenched by mom's honey-laced lemonade. Also, I ran out of cash and didn't have a job anymore." Matilda rubbed her neck. "You almost killed me with that freakin' bony elbow of yours. It should be registered as a lethal weapon. I'm just glad you didn't freakin' poke me in the eye with one of those nasty things. So who's Lori?"

Peggy wasn't sure whether to laugh or cry. She loved Tilda even though she was a magpie. Her mom used to call her Magpie Matilda since she was a toddler. On her occasional runaway episode, the house would echo with her words as if she never left. Peggy thought she'd never see Tilda again when she left so suddenly for Peru with her college mates. She figured she'd written off Texas and the family for the rest of her earthly days.

Tilda sat up and hugged her knees. She could be relentless. "You're a little old for imaginary friends, so fess up. Who's Lori?"

Sitting at the edge of the bed, Peggy turned her head and gave a deadpan stare. "An imaginary friend. Now if you insist on sharing my bed, I insist you be quiet. Welcome home." Peggy climbed under the covers and buried her head under a pillow.

"So where did you meet this imaginary friend?"

Peggy groaned. "I knew it! You just can't shut up. Okay, in a bomb shelter. I met her in a bomb shelter. She thinks it's 1955, and she appears and disappears at will. Now will you just go to sleep?"

"Aha, a time traveler. I've heard of such things in my physics class. I'm still wondering if it's true."

Peggy winced and turned a sour face toward her sister. "Are you serious?"

"Well, of course I'm serious. Okay. The map of Australia led to my adventures. If you were in Australia right now, you'd be one day older than you are now. Different time zones."

Holding the pillow over her head, Peggy gave a muffled response. "But that's just a time zone thing. We're talking sixty years! And apparently, there's some seventy-four-year-old woman who's the same person. Can you understand how crazy all of this happens to be?" Now she was practically yelling in utter frustration through the pillow case.

"Aha!" said the rambling Tilda. "You say you met her in a bomb shelter? It could be a wormhole. They exist according to many scientific theories. They are something like black holes. It's possible she's traveling to and from wherever she is now to that space before. Maybe there's some energy force going on in that dugout."

Peggy bolted up from beneath the fabric. "How ludicrous!"

"Oh no, jello-for-brains sister of mine! It's all about transmission events and reception events allowing someone to move backward and forward in time. And how do you know she's where she is at seventy-four when she's with you? Maybe she's going back and forth. Have you ever met the old lady Lori?"

"Not yet. Look, this is all way too confusing, and I don't want to think about it right now! Good night, Tilda. And if Lori shows up, tell her to stay the hell in the future, I mean present, or wherever I'm not!"

"Wow! You're an angry little dudette, aren't you? Mark my words. You have a time traveler on your hands." Tilda preferred Matte as her moniker, and she'd made that known several times to her younger sibling. She wondered if Peggy simply forgot or called her Tilda to hurt her feelings. She kicked Peggy's behind with her barefoot and blurted, "You know I hate Matilda and, especially now, Tilda, and you still call me that name. What's your problem?"

"Right now, you're my problem." Peggy understood that there was practically no way of silencing the magpie, even if she wasn't prattling senseless gossip or idle chatter as most magpies were inclined to do. She peered at her sister with imploring eyes, a roadmap of weariness.

"Matte begins with an M. It's simple as that. Tilda is with a T, Matte is with an M. Everything, everyone in this freakish house has an M. Get it?" She barely blinked as she fixated on her sister, hoping to penetrate the super-sized ego and self-centeredness of the Mitchell tribe's self-proclaimed vagabond.

Tilda softened and smiled at her beleaguered bed mate. "Yeah, I get it Peggy with a P." Drawing her knees back to her chest, she resumed where they started, bringing their encounter to a full circle. "Why don't you just visit the old lady and tell her to stop vexing you?"

"Believe me, I intend to. I have something she wants." Peggy smirked, even if unaware because deep inside, she resented her circumstances leading her on narrow paths not of her own choices. A full-mouth, face-stretching yawn punctuated her final attempt to conclude their inadvertent, unintended parley. "Now please, go to sleep or go away!"

Matilda, a.k.a. Tilda, a.k.a. Matte, was dead asleep, snoring only slightly but loud enough to keep Peggy awake in her random cerebrations. Peggy woke to a pitch-black room even though the shades were rolled up and the curtains drawn back awaiting the hazy light of dawn. Her digital clock blinked 4:12 a.m. She was surprised she got any sleep at all with the slumbering Tilda still by her side. A bird chirped a blithe little tune that gave her some crazy sense of hope for the new day. She peered out the window, noticing her father's truck already gone.

She wondered if he missed his baseball team–sized family when he was on the road. "He's a good provider," repeated his mom with a blessing at every meal. Head bowed upon finishing the traditional prayer, she whispered, "God bless your dad. He's a good provider." Every now and then, she would add, "And for a special intention."

Miriam, her curiosity and precocious manner alighted, said bluntly, "Why are you blessing him? He only causes trouble when he's here."

"Well dear," said her mother with a beaming face, "because he provides the meal. He is the one who puts the food on our table."

Tilda was stirring, and Peggy wished she would sleep for another hour or so, not wanting to engage in any further banter. She silently berated herself for spilling out her story like the guts of a fish being filleted. Her only placation was that Tilda would most likely be gone in a week's time due to her restless spirit and wandering ways. She heard mumbling directed to her and felt prompted to respond, "What?"

"Time machine. Some countries have already developed one. She must be a time machine experiment."

"Go back to sleep, Tilda. You're dreaming again." Peggy returned to thoughts of Jack Mitchell, the provider. She peered at the empty driveway. By now, he'd be watching the sunrise on the road, hands gripping the wheel, ten and two, like he told her once when he let her drive his truck.

"Keep your hands on ten and two. Think of the wheel as a clock, Peggy." He called her Peggy, which repeatedly endeared him to her when he was sober. He understood why she preferred not to be called Margaret. "Too many Ms in this house. It's the house of M's."

Although, she never understood why he didn't come up with a few suggestions of his own for names. Mary Mitchell didn't own a car. She felt it was better to walk or take public transportation to her destinations. Many times, her brood of children managed to buy a vehicle for a few hundred bucks and run family errands. Next in line was Michael, biding his time to obtain a license. He'd already saved up $1,000 in the last few years to buy a car. Once again, the driveway would have another four wheels instead of the emptiness resulting from Jack Mitchell's road trips.

"Peggy, what time is it?" Tilda sounded phlegmy and tired, maybe sick and tired.

"Four thirty." Peggy drew the curtains forward. "Dear Lord, what's up with you? Go to sleep, will you?"

Tilda turned her achy, feverish body to the door, away from her wide-awake roommate. Beads of sweat formed on her brow, and she succumbed to the flu she'd been fighting.

"Do you really think this Lori is traveling through time?" Peggy turned her head. Tilda was asleep again even though tossing and turning. Peggy listened to her sister's ragged breathing in the pitch-black room. She quietly left and closed the door. Walking through the unlit hallway, she made her way to Miriam's room in hopes that her youngest sister would take in a weary soul.

"Is that you, Peggy?" The little voice came from under sheets. "Don't be mad. I have your doll with me."

"What are you doing awake, dipster?" Peggy had more names for the Mitchell clan than she would bother counting. Whatever came out, so be it. Peggy adjusted her eyes and noticed a hint of the gold robes adorning the boy king. "Aha, I wouldn't give it to you, so you took it anyway."

"Don't you remember? You told me I could have it." The little face appeared angelic, soft, round, and wide-eyed with innocence, even if devilish at times.

"Move over, midget. I need a solid hour of sleep. I'm exhausted."

"Peggy, do you know why she's here?" Miriam barely mouthed as if thoughts of the unearthly creature would conjure her up.

"No, frog face, I haven't a clue. I'm not sure she even knows." Peggy closed her eyes, and moments later, a deep slumber took over.

Miriam felt under her pillow for the soft feather she kept as a victory over an enemy and like a little warrior confronting her greatest fear. The infant statue was now her shield and protector. Comforted by Peggy's soft whistle of a snore, she smiled and made her way back to her dream world.

Tilda's fever broke by Saturday morning, but the day was tortuous for Mary Mitchell who beat a path back and forth for ice chips, ginger ale, dry toast, and thermometer checks. Tilda was never one for suffering through a malady without bringing hostages, that much Peggy remembered about her sister's childhood. Even though they were a few years apart, she recalled the time Tilda sprained her wrist and carried on for weeks about not being able to do homework, chores, or basically live her life. At twenty, she hadn't changed much when it came to suffering, and the butt of her misery now was the bedroom's owner.

"So tell me the story while I lay here dying in your bed, string bean." Tilda had a penchant for off-the-cuff nicknames, a small trait they both shared as if it had a genetic quality.

"First, tell me why you're here. What happened in Peru?" Peggy wrapped a hand-embroidered white linen handkerchief in front of her face to protect her orifices from the germ-ridden plague of a sister.

"Peru and I didn't get along. I saw the sites and was ready to leave. I told you, jungle rot is not my preferred form of penance in life. I much rather suffer through you and the Mitchell family in general." Tilda hung her forearm over her forehead to get a quick read on her condition. "I'm burning up, man. Can you get mom in here? I don't think I'll last much longer. I think I see the white light coming my way." Lowering her arm, she added, "Speaking of white light, how did your time traveler first appear to you? Did she just throw herself into your path?"

"Pretty much. You know, I really don't want to talk about it anymore. I'm kind of sorry I even brought it up." Peggy adjusted her mummy wrappings.

"Don't worry, I won't tell anyone. Who would believe me? It's like you're smoking crack or something. That's what most of my friends would think. Of course, I could tell Mom.

"You tell Mom, and you'll be dead before the flu kills you. Plus, you're not dying, you're such a wimp. Big sister with her big plans and gypsy lifestyle. You're more like a boomerang. The further out you go, the quicker you return." Peggy plopped in her fuzzy yellow bean bag resembling a blob version of Big Bird.

"Nice way to treat the dying," replied Tilda, burying her head under a pillow.

"You're not dying," said Peggy, hugging her knees. "You'll probably outlive all of us."

"You've got the bedside manner of a grizzly bear. So would you please get Mom in here?"

A soft knock on the door and Miriam crept in. "Why did you leave and not tell me?" She looked directly at a beleaguered Peggy and walked toward her, ignoring Tilda hidden in a bundle of crumpled sheets.

"Here," she continued, holding out the Infant of Prague. "I don't want it anymore. She'll come looking for it."

Curiosity got the best of the tightly wrapped Tilda, and she peeked from under her self-imposed burial cloth. "Let me see!"

"I'm not coming near you, Tildy. You're too sick." Miriam backed away.

"Okay fine, I can see from here. That doll looks like an antique. I'm guessing it's worth about one thousand, at least six hundred, at the very least. You should hock it. That's what I would do." Tilda fell back and stared at the ceiling. "You could buy me a car."

"I thought you were dying?" said Peggy dryly. "Here, give it over, Miriam. I'll keep it, since it's mine anyway." She held the religious icon and looked over at Tilda. "I'm not selling it, so don't get any ideas." Springing up from the fuzzy yellow blob, she attempted a tender expression directed toward her sister, half asleep and soaked in sweat. "Looks like you're fever's breaking. I'll go get Mom."

By Saturday night, Tilda was gone. Not dead, just gone. Once her fever broke, she felt one hundred percent, if not better, and her wanderlust kicked in like never before. She left a note saying she had some money in her wallet, and her Visa card was in good shape. She called an unnamed friend who stopped by and picked her up with plans to go back to college and resume her studies, but not in Peru. She would tell the administrators that she was near death with a fever and had to return home, not all untrue, but would definitely weave the story to her advantage.

No Lori sighting took place on Saturday, but Peggy was confident that she would arrive in time for Sunday's promised church outing. Peggy dreaded the visit. She had no inclination of stepping foot into the worship space and felt resentful for being tricked into attending. She waited until about nine that evening to break the news to her mother.

"Mom, looks like I'm going to mass with you," she said while fixing a bowl of chocolate chip mint ice cream.

"Well, that's nice, sweetheart. We're leaving at eight thirty."

Peggy stopped in mid-scoop. "You're not shocked?"

"What would you like me to say?" Mary looked up from her knitting project and peered out of crookedly placed bifocals.

Pulling open the freezer door, Peggy tossed the near-empty container into its darker recesses. "So Tilda made her escape? Why did she even bother coming home?"

"Not sure. She was very sick. I hope she knows what she's doing." Mary set the needles and emerald green wool on her lap and stared away as if trying to remember details of last night's dream. Peggy bit into the frozen confection and examined her spoon for remnants.

"Since when did Tildy ever know what she was doing? She's totally three sheets to the wind! She'll never change!"

"That's not true, Peggy. People can change. Never give up on the power of the spirit."

"Well, I'm glad to have the room back to myself. Later." Peggy walked down the hallway, licking the metal spoon while chocolate chips swirled into the green puddle of melting confection.

"Peggy. I'm glad you're going with us tomorrow. I'm really glad. Good night."

Glancing back, she eyed her mom who always looked so sad and happy all at once. Joyful sorrow. She must have lots on her mind with all these kids. Peggy considered her mom's life as dismal, like a prison guard with the inmates slowly being released after doing time. On many occasions, she wondered if her mom liked being mom and a mom so many times over. She force-fed her faith life on them. Whether it made a lasting impression or not, only time would tell even though Maria and Monica, the godly twins, seemed to be holding onto their religion. For others, such as Peggy and Tilda, it fell upon hearts not open to the message. She wasn't even sure what the message was other than attend mass, pray, and go to confession. Oh yes, and read the Bible, pray more, and do works of charity. All of her instruction sounded like a life sentence, not creative or adventurous, or even all that holy. If nothing else, Peggy remained slightly curious of her mom's consistency. *Maybe there's something to the consistency*, she thought.

Peggy fell into her bed fitted with newly washed sheets of powder blue and a vivid sunflower-print bedspread. No traces of Tilda remained behind, she who appeared like a black cloud out of nowhere. Even so, Peggy was always delighted to see her sister, actually any of her siblings on their random returns. Someday, she would leave the nest, as her mother would say, but the thought of it terrified her, especially now that she was flunking most of her classes, building a life of delinquency, and spiraling downward into depression.

She waited most of the afternoon for a visit from Lori, but for naught. By early evening, she even whispered her name aloud as if she could conjure her up. In a childish vein, she lifted up the Infant of Prague, dressed in its royal robes, and said in a singsong voice, "Oh, Lori, aren't you going to visit with your little Savior?" Still nothing. Then she got angry at herself for even the notion of missing this pesky time traveler, bilocator, or projection of her own imagination.

"I'm crazy," she uttered while regarding herself in the mirror. "Admit it, Peggy, you're crazy." She opened the medicine cabinet in search of the aspirin bottle that hid a small stash of weed. *Getting high would just make me more depressed*, she thought. *What I need is a jolt of happiness. Why isn't there a drug to make me happy?* Everything she experimented with, even prescription drugs, just created a major letdown and feeling of malaise. She giggled to herself. *Maybe Lori is my happy drug. I conjured her up to amuse myself.* Closing the cabinet, she looked again in the mirror, noticing the slightest of brown shading under her eyes. *I need some rest, that's it.* She looked dreadful, like someone troubled, nervous, and out of sync with the world. Detached and ultimately disenchanted, she immediately felt a pressure crushing into her chest, her eardrums pulsed with the whoosh of blood circulating through her body, her hands became clammy, cold, and numb. "My God, I'm having a heart attack," she cried silently. "I'm too freakin' young for a heart attack."

Barely catching her breath, she practically crawled to bed to lie down to avoid fainting in the bathroom. Pressing her face against the pillow, she took long, deep breaths, trying to stay calm and relaxed. A voice inside her murmured a prayer petition, a simple, "Please, God, help me, I don't want to die." A few minutes later, after a constant pleading, she recognized what had occurred. She had her first panic attack. All of her fears surfaced at once and caused a great strain on her physical body. After a few more deep breaths, she kept still and listened while her breathing returned to normal, the crushing weight on her chest dissipated, and her hands were dry and warm.

She looked over at the statue with the childlike, innocent face, even if inscrutable, holding the world like a weightless blue ball circled in gold. His other hand held fingers in a sign of peace. A residue of anger and disappointment welled up again. "What do I owe you?" She hissed inside the depths of her being.

The answer came so swiftly it caught her by surprise: "A visit."

23

Truth and Consequences

Light streamed into Peggy's room, adding brilliance to the oversized printed sunflower petals covering her bedspread. She sprung up to check the time and realized she had twenty minutes to get ready. She raced into the shower and sudsed up her hair and body with an all-purpose gardenia scented cleanser hanging from the overhead spout. In three minutes, she was drying off and, in less than five, heading toward the living room area.

Mary Mitchell was reclining in her absent husband's favorite chair. She looked up from her palm-sized leather-bound Bible challenging her middle daughter's frown with a good morning grin. "Well, here you are!"

Peggy stomped into the room, searching for her boots she was certain she kicked off the other night. "Thanks for waking me up, Mom. I really appreciate all the support I get around here."

"I knew you'd make it. I didn't want to push the matter." Mary closed up her book and zipped the sides together.

In renewed exasperation, Peggy ceased her search. "Since when?" she said in shrill reply.

Mary's grin undiminished, she reached down next to the recliner and picked up a pair of cocoa brown fake suede boots. "I believe these are yours?"

Peggy rudely snatched the boots, plopped down on the nearby gray velour sofa, and jammed her heels into the footwear. Stamping her feet into the carpet, she lifted herself up and made a proclamation. "Okay, let's go."

Mary peeked at her wristwatch. "We have ten minutes, and the others are still getting ready. Why don't you see what's keeping Miriam? She's usually waiting for everyone else."

Nothing in my life was going as planned, thought Peggy. *I'm giving up this precious time to myself when everyone is out of the house at church, and I can revel in my slumber or download a movie and eat a bowl of ice cream with crumbled bacon on top*. She remembered how her mom stopped imploring her to come to church about two years ago. She did everything but drag her out of the house but finally gave up and gave in. At that moment, Miriam stepped in the room, surprised to see her sister awake and joining them.

"You're coming with us? Are you bringing your friend? Is she here?"

Drawing a finger to her lips, she responded. "Quiet, little mouse, now's not the time! Let's just go." Peggy did not expect Lori to accompany her on the long walk to church. She wished one of her older siblings was home with a car to drive the exhausting journey. Only twenty minutes, but it felt like an eternity as she dragged her feet while staring down at the gravel road.

Her mom prayed the rosary the entire way, which annoyed Peggy to no end since she was given the duty of holding Miriam's hand. She visualized shaking a fist at her now invisible tormentor. Scanning behind and to each side, she anticipated an appearance yet nothing or no one materialized. For a second or two, she contemplated turning back, but she had gone too far, and the church bells rang as she entered with her mom, Michael, the Marty twins, and Miriam still by her side. Light streamed through stained glass windows with a mosaic reflection of primary colors spilling across the polished wooden pews. Organ music filled the space with a variety of instrument sounds resembling an ensemble with flutes, drums, and piano. A cantor was warming up the congregation with a celebratory hymn of praise and thanksgiving. Sitting at the pew's end, Peggy scanned her surroundings for a final time and saw faces of classmates checking or sending text messages, young mothers attempting to amuse or quiet their small children, elderly couples dressed in their finery, and no sign of Lori. She did a double take of every young girl roughly between the ages of twelve and fifteen until it became obvious to her mom that she was distracted and not giving full attention to the start of mass. A tug on her sleeve ceased the ogling of the environment minus the sole reason for her being there.

Utterly exasperated, she fixed her gaze upon the Infant of Prague over near the exit to the church hall on the lower level. The statue was dressed in a purple velvet cape and satin tunic of the same color. He held the familiar white and gold orb, and the two fingers of his other small hand were held up in a peace sign. One more furtive look for Lori among the congregation yet no sign of her. *A trick to get me here*, she mused. But why, she could not fathom. A lithe, young woman with sleek blond hair approached the ambo and greeted the congregation.

"Good morning and welcome to the Church of the Holy Child. A special greeting to all visitors, and we hope you come back again."

Peggy felt the lector was glaring at her even though the chirpy blonde's mouth was turned up into a warm smile. *I'm being paranoid*, she thought, *and why not? I don't belong here. I don't even want to be here. I've been tricked, duped, fooled, conned, double-crossed, betrayed, bamboozled, and abandoned.* The litany of negative words and thoughts built to a crescendo throughout the entire opening hymn "O Come, O Come Emmanuel" and the priest's entrance and comfortable stance in front of the altar.

"Let us pray," he began, and the liturgy commenced.

Peggy sunk into the pew, wishing she could vaporize or exit without notice. Feeling trapped, she surrendered to the priest's words, the scripture readings, the kneeling, sitting and standing, and finally, the raising of the bread and cup. As a child, she was always distracted throughout the mass, seated while stretching her twiglike lower extremities attempting to reach the back of the pew in front of her. When her mother offered her the sign of peace with a kiss and hug, Peggy jerked away. Her anger was welling up, and tears brimmed her eyes.

Mary looked at her forlorn daughter and smiled. "Peace, Peggy darling." She looked at her mom's serene expression and broke down to allow a reassuring hug. "You're okay," she whispered in Peggy's ear.

It's not okay. I'm choking here, on my own self-pity, Peggy told herself while hiding behind an emotionless mask.

Her mother hugged each one of the Mitchells with a gesture of peace, while Peggy took one more sweeping survey in search of Lori. *Maybe she wants to surprise me*, she thought. Disappointed for a final time, she knelt while the sacrificial meal, the body and blood, was lifted in the hands of the priest. He was from India, which she had discerned from the homily, the little bit that she listened to with resignation. She remained behind with Miriam while the family lined up to receive Holy Communion. She rested her head in her hands and felt the weight of something, maybe sin, pressing down upon her. At that moment, Miriam put a small hand on her back as a gesture of comfort. She peeked at her sister who was transfixed, her eyes on the altar. Leaving the church after mass, Peggy refused to acknowledge any of her peers or acquaintances. Becky Sims, a schoolmate who attempted to befriend her the first day she arrived from Indiana, would not be easily dissuaded.

Rebuffed with a slight nod for a good morning greeting, she persisted. "Hi, Peggy, how's it going?" Becky tried to keep step with the recalcitrant classmate.

"I'm kind of in a hurry," blurted Peggy.

Glancing back to the thinning congregation, Becky remarked, "But your family is still—"

"Well, I have to be somewhere." Peggy interrupted, looking straight ahead.

"Any place where I can join you?" Becky was indefatigable, at best, which amused Peggy.

Coming to an abrupt halt, she noticed the freckled, upturned nose resembled Lori's. Even the strawberry blonde hair wavy and loose as it framed her heart-shaped face. "You're not getting a clue. I really just want to be alone."

"Oh, I'm sorry," said Becky, attempting to be cheerful. "Maybe next week or something. Enjoy the day." She waved and disappeared into the remaining crowd, running to catch up with family members and kind of leaving Peggy in her dust and lingering thoughts.

"Was that? No! Now I'm really ready for the psyche ward!"

Miriam ran up to her out of breath. "Why did you leave us?"

"I figured you'd be staying. I want to get home."

"You were looking for her, huh?" Miriam said as the other Mitchells approached.

"Maybe." Peggy shrugged, kicking a little rock loose from the gravel surface.

"Maybe she was there, and you couldn't see her." Miriam wiped her runny nose on the soft sleeve of her pink felt coat. Most articles of her clothing were one shade or another of pink on her insistence.

"You should ask for a tissue, little miss lime green jello for brains," smirked Peggy.

"Do you have one?" Miriam was still caught up in her predicament.

"No," answered Peggy.

Mary Mitchell noticed her youngest daughter's smeary face and retrieved a tissue from her coat pocket. "Here, darling, wipe your nose."

Miriam reached for the tissue, while her mom was distracted by a neighbor coming up and inviting them all over for brunch next Sunday, the last week of Advent.

"Anyway," whispered Miriam. "I think I heard her wings fluttering. I hear wings in church."

Peggy looked at the cleaned up urchin with the blue marble eyes earnestly peering at her. "So how do you know they were hers?"

She reached in her pocket. "I found this."

Peggy briefly examined the feather. "Big deal, a feather."

"Same as the one I found in my room." Miriam skipped ahead as Peggy stared back into her thoughts and catalog of Lori images.

"Look, I'm a bird. I can fly!" cried Miriam with newfound mirth.

Peggy, even in her gloomy state, chuckled at Miriam's burst of energy. A spark of cheeriness touched her soul, and as much as she preferred wallowing in her melancholia, an irrepressible gratitude took hold.

24

True Confessions

Father O'Malley's inflamed knees ached with the deepening chill and rising humidity. Countless times, he had hands clasped on those caps while listening to confessions, straining to hear the whispered sins of the very young and slightly recoiling from the loud recounting of misdeeds from the hard-of-hearing elderly. With clasped hands, he concentrated more on his prayers, not the appropriate posture for an instrument of God's healing power. He would remind himself how essential it was to stay open and listen to the penitent heart and the hands-on-knee posture kept him focused on the confessor. Some days, he felt like the sideline coach of the football team and other days, like the quarterback coming up with the game plan. He knew he needed to confide a path of reparation so crucial to amend sinful acts. Rarely severe, always loving, but direct, he was exacting, at times. Peggy's penance was one of those times.

Palms bracing knees, he gave instruction. "Give back to those you've stolen from, in some way. For your penance, say three Hail Mary's and make a good act of contrition."

25

Back to the Well

The following day, a Sunday visit, Father O'Malley played his usual role of mediator, this time between a reluctant visitor Peggy and the vaguely disoriented resident of the assisted living facility. The accompanying facility manager, Floyd Rodgers, filled in the backstory.

"Well, she didn't come in here until about two years ago. Yeah, it was in September 2013. Her records show she started talking about people from her past that died long ago. She talked to them as if they were here. Her mom, dad. We weren't sure what the problem was, but then a friend gave us all the details. How her mom and dad died in a tornado storm."

A heavy set woman, Nurse Clara, clutched her clipboard like a protective shield and added to the account, "So 2013, that was the year of some of the worst tornadoes we've seen in these parts." Tightening up her hair knot, she continued, "Yeah, they kind of tied it to the Moore, Oklahoma, storm. She was visiting a friend and saw that twister right up front and close from what I hear. Not too many people see a level 5, you know, and live to talk about it."

Father O'Malley remembered all the news of that day. A massive tornado tore through the flat plains, a monumental, swirling mass of madness. On May 20, the maelstrom—phenomenal in its proportions with a twenty-mile path of destruction—touched down in Oklahoma City, Oklahoma. The devastation started the prior day, hundreds of homes damaged or destroyed with little or no resistance to the 200 mph winds. Lori, as fate would have it, was spending the week with an old friend from her hometown of

Lubbock, Texas. A retired school teacher, Tally (short for Talia) lived now in the suburban town of Moore, Oklahoma. Lori had never been to Moore, usually visiting her friend in Oklahoma City where Tally taught math at Bishop McGuiness High School.

Two years ago, after prolonging her decision to retire, Tally decided to pick up roots again and leave any remnants of urban life, at least Oklahoma's version of it, and seek out quieter streets and less housing. What she didn't realize was the remarkable prescience she exhibited by purchasing a house with an underground storm shelter beneath a two-car garage. Now a widow, she certainly did not need the two-car garage, but she felt safer with the shelter. *You never know*, she thought, *with the crazy weather, anything's possible.* She rallied and protested against global warming trends created by mass consumption of fossil fuels and a depleted ozone wreaking havoc on coastlines with fierce hurricanes, flat plains with twisters, and just life in general on planet Earth. She and Lori would argue the point, with Lori pointing out that America alone could do little, if nothing, to stem the course.

"Tally, for every coal mine we close down, three more are starting up somewhere in China."

"I can't control the world, Lori, but I can make a difference here in my homeland." Tally would counter while they sipped coffee from oversized mugs and picked at a fresh batch of monkey bread, a truly addictive conglomeration of dough, sugar, cinnamon, nuts, butter, and a caramel glaze.

It was one of those visits and conversations uncannily precipitating the May 20 storm that swept through the countryside so suddenly yet was so large in size that the two women could see its approach from a large picture window. For Lori, it was living out what happened to her parents nearly sixty years ago while she slept in her bunker. Frozen by the haunting, horrendous visual, a furtive, sorrowful part of her wanted to be swept up by the storm. She experienced, on the very fringe of fright or flight, a ludicrous notion of the beloved heroine Dorothy from the *Wizard of Oz* sitting on her bed in a swirling house as barn animals and farm debris flew about in her inner circle, the eye of the tunnellike storm. She thought maybe she would see her family, her mom baking chicken pot pie, inspecting with deep admiration her buttery, golden, flaky pastry crust, the pride of Lubbock. Her dad would be determining the last few words of a crossword puzzle, his version of relaxation on a Sunday afternoon.

Tally shrieked and got no response from a transfixed Lori. She tugged at her friend's white cotton sweater, nearly ripping it off her shoulder. "Let's go, Lori! The shelter under my garage. Let's go!" She shook her friend in wild exasperation.

"I can't. I won't go underground. Just leave me here, please!" Lori sat, motionless.

"Are you freakin' crazy? Stop it now. Get on your feet and follow me, or by God, I'll pull you out of here by your hair." Tally was frantic, not expecting such an irrational response from her dear friend. With the strength of a woman half her age, she pulled Lori off the chair and dragged her out of the kitchen. "I swear I'll kick your ass to get you down those stairs. Dear God," added Tally, "this is a level 5, I just know it. If you stay here, it's suicide, you idiot."

Lori was overcome by Tally's strength, like that of an ox with the surges of adrenaline igniting every fiber of her being. Forcing Lori, like a beaten captive, Tally pushed her down the stairs of the shelter and latched them in within mere moments of the deadly storm that killed twenty-four people, injured hundreds more, and left thousands without power, or more definitively, without homes. Tally's ranch house was obliterated, and they emerged to a scene all too familiar to Lori, more vulnerable to her memories than even she could predict.

Tally's anger subsided when she witnessed her friend almost catatonic while sifting through the debris as if it was her home and her belongings in the fruitless search. And it was her home, in hidden recesses, eclipsed or hidden for so long and now ignited and fired synapses confusing the where and when and clarifying the millisecond of being orphaned. Tally bit her lip, wiped grime and tears from Lori's distraught face, and hugged her with a motherly embrace.

"I'm sorry I was so mean and downright nasty. You scared me so much, Lori."

Lori blinked twice as slow as a normal person. Shock had taken over, and Tally began recognizing the signs. She wrapped her friend in a blanket and called 911.

* * *

Peggy sat with the box of buttons sitting on her lap suddenly at a loss for any meaningful conversation. She waited for the stranger to notice the small objects purloined so many decades ago. With pleasantries aside, they grasped at some common ground. "Yes, Joy. I knew about your friend, Joy."

Lori Hopkins, appearing shriveled beyond her seventy-four years, dabbed at her eyes that tended to tear up without provocation. "She died the day of the tornado." A second dab, and she peered into the folds of her hanky embroidered with yellow flowers competing with the dingy, overly used cloth of nearly a similar shade. "I never forgave my grandma for letting me go back to school without knowing." The young Lori that Peggy met had no knowledge of Joy's death.

She had asked her fleetingly during one of their park walks, "So do you have any friends?" Peggy picked at a small scab on her wrist, most likely an old cut from hopping a fence or running through some brush. She sat silently, recalling the conversation.

"I have one really close friend, Joy."

"Joy? Sure you're not making her up? I mean it's not like you're real anyway." Peggy provoked the savvy spirit by endlessly questioning her existence.

"She's the last person I saw before I fell asleep. She came to visit me."

Peggy preferred not coaxing along the disheveled figure sitting across from her in the simply decorated room with one bed, one nightstand, and one set of drawers. The curtains adorning one window were lime green, of all colors, resembling bile or some other substance from deep within the gut. She also deplored prompting her to conjure up long-forgotten memories. She simply desired to leave the buttons behind and get on with her own presently disheveled life. Even so, there was another pull deep inside her that sought to explore and understand the lonely, forgotten soul's story and why on God's earth she was sent to her.

Not knowing what possessed her, she boldly proclaimed, "Yes, I met you when you were fourteen. You fixed up a bomb shelter into a Christmas room and spent hours in it. You even had a working television."

The woman sitting in the high-backed chair upholstered, with a worn and soiled beige cloth and flat wooden armrests, kept very still and uttered no words. Any sane, rational person would immediately blurt out, "Nonsense! Who are you, and what sort of game are you playing, missy?" Instead, she sat there with a reflective gaze as if reliving scenes in her head. Finally, after about three minutes of silence, she acknowledged Peggy and inquired, "How old are you?"

"Fourteen," said Peggy, offering no further conversation. Another few minutes went by, and Peggy felt anxiety and impatience rising within her.

Finally, Lori engaged again, with the mere hint of a smile or some sad attempt at one. "So you found it. I haven't been there since I was fourteen." Quite lucidly, she continued, "My parents died that Christmas year while I was tucked away safely and unaware. I fell asleep after Joy left."

"And you've not been back?" Peggy was surprised by the woman's coherence, especially since she expected an invalid with dementia who would barely acknowledge a visitor.

Relaxing a bit, she allowed the elderly Lori to speak her mind. "Only in my dreams. Many times, I'll still wake up in the darkness of my Christmas room, wondering why the world seemed so alarmingly quiet." Sliding out of her recollections, Lori readjusted her focus on the strange, gangly girl sitting across from her. "And who are you?"

"I'm Peggy. As I said, I met you—the former you—in your shelter."

"But that's impossible. Who sent you?" Lori instantly appeared frazzled and greatly perturbed.

Peggy saw it coming. There's no way a sane person would buy her story, which made even less sense now that she was confronted by the real Lori. "I know it makes no sense." Peggy felt like a third grader in the school principal's office, attempting to explain her fifth late slip or some other compromised rule. "At first, I thought I imagined you, but you are real and the Lori in the shelter…well, she's real."

Lori shook her head slowly. "No, I don't believe so. You must be dreaming her up. It makes no sense." Lori reached for her buzzer, and a sonorous voice came over the intercom.

"Yes, Ms. Hopkins."

"Would you please escort this young lady out? Our visit is over." She gave Peggy a stony expression. "I don't know what kind of game you're playing, but I want no part of it."

Peggy sat in utter disbelief at the turn of events. She was really hoping to find some peace of mind, some closure at their meeting, and everything was upside-down and topsy-turvy. She thought she held the winning cards and now realized she could be easily dismissed by the wave of a hand.

"Look, I'll go if you want, but I'm really here to give back something. Here." She extended her hands with the box of buttons. "These are yours, and, from what I can tell, it's the reason you appeared to me in the first place. I stooped down to pick them up, and you appeared out of thin air." Peggy felt honest-to-goodness goose bumps rising. "I'll never forget it."

Lori stared at the box, not touching it. "My buttons. Her buttons." An outpouring of emotions rippled across her face. Peggy broke through the wall and prepared for the aftermath.

A burly yet pleasant nurse's aide entered the room. His carnation pink uniform added vibrancy to the beige-on-beige milieu. "Ms. Hopkins, you tired?" Nurse Mike turned to look at the pale, super thin teen bent over hugging her knees.

"Mike, I've changed my mind. Give us about fifteen minutes?"

"Okay, Ms. Hopkins. I'll be back with the good priest. He's making his rounds, and he'll be here before he leaves."

"He better be since he's my ride," Peggy said in a defiant tone.

"Mind your manners, little Miss Malcontent. She giving you trouble, Ms. Hopkins?"

Lori raised her eyebrows. "You wouldn't believe me if I told you. Are you hungry…I'm sorry, I forgot your name."

"It's Peggy, and yes, I am hungry, but I wouldn't eat any food in here."

"Help yourself to the snack machine. Looks like you don't eat too healthy anyway," Mike quipped.

"Bring her a protein shake, would you please, Mike? The good one with the frozen strawberries." Lori settled back into her chair, and Mike walked out, whistling a version of *Yankee Doodle Dandy*.

"Why the change of heart?" Peggy felt a strain of relief of not being dismissed. She felt a connection to the senior Lori, even if tenuous.

"Because if anything would get a reaction out of me, it would be these buttons. Did I tell you what they were?"

Peggy felt the shift again, and this time, toward a rather prodigious form of trust. "They belong to your mom, and you were going to give them to her for Christmas."

"Yes, I guess you would know if you're telling the truth. No one could have told you that, at least not anyone alive to my knowledge."

Mike, respecting their privacy, knocked lightly on the door before entering.

"Yes, come on in," said Lori, eliciting a slight spasm of coughing. "Well that was quick," she said while reaching for her yellowed hanky.

Mike paraded into the room with a drink nearly as pink as his uniform. "I put some extra strawberries in here." He winked and presented the health shake to Peggy with a slight bow.

"How do you know I'm not allergic to strawberries?" she said with her usual smirk and penchant for testing of her surroundings and the people in her path.

"Just drink it up. It's loaded with vitamins, and you'll feel like a million bucks," said Lori with a new coughing spasm.

"Doesn't seem to be working for you. I can't believe you're Lori. You were so…young!" Peggy took a swallow of the drink, allowing the frothy mixture to linger around her semi-pursed lips.

"Weren't we all once," added Mike, fluffing up a pillow on Lori's hospital bed. "Ms. Hopkins is our favorite. She doesn't give us any trouble."

"Thank you, Mike. I'll let you know when we're done with our little private session." Lori adjusted herself on the now-uncomfortable chair as she stretched her legs in front of her to improve circulation. Mike made a slight bow and left only after giving Peggy a taste of her own smirk.

"So now you want me here? That was a quick turn of events."

"It's more than the buttons. There's something down there that means a lot to me, and I'm sure you may have noticed it." Lori reached behind to grab the small pillow supporting her lower lumbar. She tossed it, now an unwanted hindrance to her comfort, hitting the wall and landing on the bed.

Peggy was uncomfortable with Lori's sudden movements, impulses, changes of attitudes, and, most noticeably, aged appearance. To say she was troubled and a little freaked out by the wrinkled, faded version of the same spry, spirited, naive teen she befriended was an understatement. With her best poker face, she answered, keeping all gestures in check. Gulping the last of the pink drink, she set the glass on the floor.

"I noticed lots of things. You really junked up the place."

Lori strained to reach her nightstand, disturbing a layer of dust only noticeable in natural light. The wheels at its base moved it along ever so slightly as she reached for the drawer adding to the challenge as Peggy watched and waited without assisting her. Still unsure of the strange woman, sixty years older than the Lori she so frequently encountered, Peggy shrunk back in her chair. Lori clutched a small piece of paper tattered on every corner. The writing was smeared and blotchy, the work of a blue fountain pen.

"Are you familiar with this prayer?" Lori said, holding out the article like some sort of treasure.

Peggy, unblinking and unimpressed, replied, "Probably not."

"It's called Saint Andrew's Prayer. For those devoted to the Infant Jesus. Well, we pray it fifteen times every day from November 30 through Christmas Eve. Would you like to read it?"

With her best eye roll, Peggy took the piece of paper and read the words: "St. Andrew's Christmas Prayer, "Hail and blessed be the hour and moment in which the Son of God was born of the most pure Virgin Mary, at midnight, in Bethlehem, in piercing cold. In that hour, vouchsafe, O my God! to hear my prayer and grant my desires, through the merits of Our Saviour Jesus Christ, and of His Blessed Mother. Amen."

Peggy read the words twice. A short prayer, one evoking hope as much as she hated to admit, even if silently.

"Among all the decorations I hauled down there, I had one special little treasure. A statue."

"I know, I know. Yes, we battled over that one too." Now Peggy felt like the nourishing beverage was working like a truth serum, or maybe it was the presence of this old lady with her piercing, hazel-colored eyes and direct gaze.

"Do you have it now?" Leaning forwarded, she looked a little comical in an effort to intimidate the brusque and impenetrable youth.

"Why would I have it with me?" said Peggy in a capricious manner.

"Well, if your intention was to return anything you took that belonged to me, like these buttons, then you would have it with you, right?"

Peggy had to chuckle to herself at the medical minds who deemed this woman suffering from dementia. *If she doesn't have her wits about her, then we're all doomed*, she thought. Visions of Father O'Malley played across her mind screen with his confessor's words, "Give back to those you've stolen from in some way." In this way, it would have to be direct, no substitutes, and she felt exposed once again for a defect in her new makeup, the one that wouldn't lie, or steal, or cheat. Oh, if it were only so easy. A slice of her psyche wanted to play this one out and keep the now-imposing senior citizen from gaining any ground. A simple, "Nope, don't know what you're talking about," begged to emerge from devilish lips, for no other reason than to create confusion and discord.

Peggy stretched out her lanky limbs, cocked her head, and smiled broadly at Lori. "I gave your infant statue to my little sister, Miriam. Actually, she took it before I gave it to her. So it's not mine any longer, and I never, in a million years, expected to meet you in the flesh."

"Miriam, my mother's name."

"My mother's aunt's name, by marriage."

Now came the ace up her sleeve, what she was waiting to drop like a bomb, no not in a shelter but in a verbal ambush. "You see, Lori. We're actually related by marriage. Your mother was an only child, but she married into a large family from Boston. One of the brothers, Tom Hopkins, was my mother's uncle. My little sister, Miriam, was named after your mother. I checked it all out, did the family tree, everything I could to tie all the strings together. Even so"—slumping again, she fell back to her uncomfortable-in-her-own skin self—"it doesn't explain why in the world I would meet you in a bomb shelter. Unless it's not really you."

Lori sat limply in her chair with its ramrod back as Peggy watched for a reaction, any reaction and received nothing for her surprising, if not shocking, news. Not shocking like a sudden miracle occurring and nothing even close to what she'd been experiencing since her fateful day of stepping down into the long-forgotten shelter. Nevertheless, Peggy sat wordlessly. She really had no other startling revelation, and she, honestly, rarely engaged in small talk.

Lori gave a shrug. "Well then, welcome to the family. I hope you don't find it too lonely, there aren't many of us," she finally said while squirming a little in her chair. "I think I need to stretch these legs. Do you mind walking out in the hallway with me? You know, in case I fall over or something. My balance isn't what it used to be."

Okay, thought Peggy, *so now I'm playing nursemaid.* She gave her best harrumph and side comment. "Lonely? Lady, there are ten kids in my family. We were crawling all over each other until a year or so ago. I could use some loneliness."

"I think you've got too much loneliness. I can see it. I'm an expert in the field."

Peggy guided a stiff-legged Lori out into the hallway as she clasped the empty protein shake glass in her free hand. "What's your story? There's about sixty years of it missing."

Lori laughed as she dug a fist into her lower back. "I could use a good massage. Know anyone? They don't do anything but push pills in here and protein shakes."

"Okay, so I didn't ask about the last sixty years." Peggy approached the nurse's station where a concerned Mike looked up from a *Sports Illustrated* magazine, swimsuit edition.

"Is she kicking you out, Miss Tempest in a Teapot?" he said, flipping through the pages with disinterest.

"What are you talking about?" said Peggy with a prompt shake of her head. "I'm doing your job, numb nuts!"

"Hey, hey, hey. We don't talk like that trash mouth, little mama," he replied with heightened indignation. "You want me to throw her out of here, Ms. Hopkins? We don't have to wait for the priest to finish his rounds. She can sit outside!" he added, glaring as he gripped the empty glass. "And you're welcome!"

"Not yet," said Lori with her lack-of-reaction manner. "Her bark is worse than her bite. Plus, I just found out we're related, so I'd rather not kick out a family member. I don't have that many, you know."

Mike draped a puffy hand across a puffier cheek. "Well, what do you know? Miss—"

"Okay, no more nicknames or corny titles!" interrupted Peggy. "You're more annoying than a barrel full of Mitchells, and believe me, that ain't easy," she added.

From down the hallway, Father O'Malley's outline drew closer. "Well, look at this, a hall huddle. How are you, Lori? Did you two enjoy your visit?" He stood in front of them in his usual pose of arms folded, rocking slightly back and forth, readily catching any conversation thrown his way.

"We've barely scratched the surface," said Lori.

"'Cause I'm not closer to understanding my Lori than I was before I got here," said Peggy with renewed resignation.

"But I am your Lori, take it or leave it." Lori leaned against a chair rail separating a beige and hunter green wall, an attempt to give ambience to an extended hallway.

"Well, I can honestly admit, I didn't see a day like today happening along. Next time you visit, bring your little sister and ask her if I can see her gift."

Peggy observed the countenance of a woman who didn't appear fazed by any sort of life-altering news. After a brief moment or two of surprise and the slightest wave of confusion, Lori appeared to settle into an uncomfortable acceptance of circumstances. Maybe that was the effect of emerging so many years ago from a blissful little cocoon into her world suddenly vanished and her family, even their earthly remains, nowhere in sight.

Impishly, Peggy replied, "What makes you think I'm coming back?"

Father O'Malley pulled at his collar, annoyed at the young girl's insolence but patient as a saint himself.

"Oh, I have no idea, but you are invited. You haven't completely worn out your welcome, even if you did drag me back into a place I'd long forgotten. But in some strange way, I thank you, Peggy… that's it, right?" Lori extended a hand, the skin mottled with age yet the fingers long, straight, and youthful.

"Well then, I would say this was a charming visit, and we thank you, Lori, for obliging us. I'm sure we'll be back, at least I know I will. Would you like to receive Holy Communion now?" Father reached in his pocket for the carrying vessel holding the Eucharist.

"Yes, Father, but I'd like to go back to my room. Peggy, would you like to join us?" She leaned against Peggy as she steadied herself for a walk down the corridor, not giving her much chance to escape or utter, "No, thank you."

Peggy glanced over at Father O'Malley who offered a lopsided attempt at a smile and a nod of encouragement. "I say we all retire back to the room for prayer and communion."

As the trio walked slowly down the hallway, Lori commented, "Peggy, short for Margaret?"

Peggy chortled, "Long story there. What about you? Must have had some kind of life over sixty years."

Lori's green eyes twinkled. "Even longer story."

Entering the room, a ray of light played with the shaded room, and for a brief second, Peggy noticed the silhouette of what appeared as a wing, the very tip of it. She blinked furiously and thought, *Must have been the curtain shadow against the wall.*

* * *

On Christmas Eve, Peggy and Miriam visited Lori and brought the Infant of Prague wrapped in recycled Christmas paper from last year's presents. Mary Mitchell reused everything until it was either threadbare, torn, or trashed beyond recognition. The paper, creased and tape worn, pictured green wreaths adorned with red bows and gold Christmas balls. The contents were wholly recognizable, even under the hastily applied covering. After a rather curt introduction, a hesitant and inconceivably shy Miriam cleared her phlegmy, childish throat and said, "Here," in a barely audible voice.

Tears streamed down Lori's face—tears of joy, tears of remembrance, tears yielding to sixty years of grief. The tears continued before she could even elicit a smile or rip away the wrapping. Peggy and Miriam just sat and watched her hold the little statue close and cradle it to her chest, still clumsily sheathed in the Christmas paper.

"Aren't you going to open it?" said Miriam, impatient for her gift to be revealed.

"I know what it is, and I'm happy right now, at this moment, just holding it." She placed the present in her lap and peeled away the paper with its worn wreaths.

"Oh, I have something else for you," said Peggy, looking and feeling more awkward by the moment. It's just a card I made up. It's not really a Christmas card, but, well, here." She thrust the envelope into Lori's hands and sat back with folded arms as a shield against any reaction from its recipient.

Lori turned the envelope, opening and pulling out a handmade card with a pasted image on the front. The black-and-white photo showed a Lucy Ricardo wearing a silly hat and sillier smile and holding up a brown medicine bottle. Lori, puzzled and amused, shook her head and studied the image for a seemingly endless minute. Finally, she opened it to read the sentiment, "This probably means nothing to you, but it began my road back to health. Thanks for being there, even if you weren't."

"Well," said Lori, head tilted upward. "You're welcome."

On their way home, Miriam eyed her big sister with regard. "I've been thinking, Peggy."

"Oh, now we're in trouble. What are you thinking, Peanut?"

"The doll, I mean the baby Jesus."

"Yeah, what about it?" Peggy held out a hand and stretched her fingers wide and wiggled them as a signal.

Miriam peered down at the hand and glanced up at Peggy still gazing straight ahead into an unknown future. Miriam grasped one of the fingers and yanked hard.

"Ouch, brat! Why did you do that?" Peggy examined her assaulted extremity with a scornful expression.

"Because you're not looking at me, and I'm talking to you."

Peggy heaved a sigh and halted her quick stride. “Okay, now you have my attention. What is it?”

“Wondering about something I heard about Jesus in Sunday school this week.”

Peggy struggled to look sincere. “Wouldn’t that be every week?”

“Yes, but this time, we talked about the Second Coming. Do you know what that means?”

“Well, that’s an easy one. It means when Jesus comes again at the end of the world. Even I can answer that one.”

“I’m thinking of the baby Jesus, the doll, and the statue in church. Is that how Jesus will come back, like the boy?”

“I don’t know. Probably not. He was a grown man when he died. Does it matter?”

“But he’s God. He can do anything.”

Peggy cut to the quick, “What’s your point, Miriam?” Only on rare instances did she call her sister by her given name.

“The boy is holding a blue ball. The world. So that’s like a clue to a secret, maybe. He’ll come back and fill the sky. But he’ll be a boy, right?”

“Why does it matter? It doesn’t.” Peggy was growing uncomfortable with the line of discussion or ponderings from the adolescent mind.

“It does. He’ll be the boy in the fancy clothes.”

“How do you know, smarty pants?” Peggy’s exhaustion crept in, a tiredness from wrestling with her restless spirit and time spent in a church pew. Separating out her sins and facing the ugly truth of her actions.

“I don’t know,” said the unsuspecting child, unaware of the turmoil she created in her elder sibling. “But it’s the world he’s holding, the blue ball. He’s telling us he will be here again. Like the boy.”

“So now you’re a prophet?” Peggy couldn’t help but smile.

“What’s a prophet?”

“Okay, believe what you want, motor mouth. Let’s get home. I’m hungry and exhausted and going back to bed.”

"Peggy, I'm not afraid of your angel anymore."

Peggy stopped again. "My angel?"

"It must be your guardian angel, like the prayer." Miriam cleared her throat, squeezed her eyes shut, and clasped her hands. "Angel of God, my guardian dear, to whom God's love commits me here, ever this day, be at my side to light and guard, to rule and guide. Amen."

Succumbing to a child's reasoning, Peggy spread her arms like wings. "Okay, it's my angel, my life, my everything! How 'bout making me breakfast?"

"I'm too young to cook. Plus, I need to go to sleep before Santa comes. You can make me breakfast. I like peanut butter and jelly on toast."

"Let's go, I guess I can handle that one."

***

Two weeks later, Peggy started her new job at the Lone Star Dollar Store, once known as the Lone Star Five & Dime. She stocked shelves with January sales items, which amused her since the full price was usually one dollar and now slashed to fifty cents or less. Lots of seasonal items, scented candles, tree lights, cushy snowmen, coloring books, puzzles, and tiny boxes of chocolates were shoved into the front and center shelves for customers eyeing stocking stuffers for the next Christmas tide.

At six o'clock on a Saturday morning, she was greeted by Lily Lopez, a black-haired, black-eyed sixteen-year-old who was intent on showing her the ropes. A much calmer, more peace-filled Peggy decided against her smarmy remarks finding the shedding of old habits easier every day by adopting the discipline and imposed self-will of kind acts and expressions. She discovered that she actually did enjoy the company of people and worked on practicing this new attitude in her family dynamic, the truest test of conversion, if any! She vaguely recalled stealing trinkets off similar shelves while her mother was preoccupied, the memories now foggy and nearly as dissipated as the images of Lori that struggled to remain vivid and clear. No longer saddened by the disappearance of Lori, she still attempted some understanding of the effervescent spirit that invaded her life, or perhaps, the life she invaded in that forgotten cellar.

Father O'Malley, relying on Celtic angel folklore, won himself over with the notion that Lori's guardian angel, masked as a youthful version of her human assignment, materialized long enough to lead Peggy to the forgotten, lonely woman and bring her some form of joy before leaving this world. The theory was as good as any, and Peggy was inclined to believe in angels as messengers of God as mentioned several times in Scripture, even the mother of God on the Feast of the Annunciation, pointed out to her repeatedly during years of Bible school.

"It's ironic, isn't it?" Fran, typically searching out the cloud around the silver lining. He stopped by the day after Christmas to pay a visit and give Peggy a present. After her mom hugged him and offered a plate of Mexican wedding cakes and chocolate milk, Peggy and Fran sat and compared notes. Peggy confided that she and Lori—the current Lori—spent a handful of hours in each other's company and how the forlorn old lady was so incredibly joy-filled since having possession of her small treasure.

"I know a little about Irish traditions. I studied symbolic Celtic art before considering a tattoo. The tradition is that if you bury the Infant of Prague, you will have the blessing of good weather. In your friend's case, she buried it, in a fashion, and her family was devastated."

"But she didn't really bury it, not really. She buried herself with her case against her mom, and that wasn't even intentional. The statue was sitting there as a little shrine. So what did you buy me?"

Peggy reached for the purple velvet box sitting on the crate-like magazine table, and Fran reached for a fourth cookie. "These are pretty good," he commented, wiping spare powdered sugar on his gray cords. Opening the box, she marveled at the old-fashioned pin, a ceramic nosegay with tiny flowers of pink, purple, blue, orange, and yellow.

"It's a friendship pin."

"A friendship pin? Oh," said a speechless Peggy.

"To say, we're still friends," said Fran, polishing off his fifth Mexican wedding cake.

"Well, of course we are. Thanks, it's…different," replied Peggy, deciding on a cake herself.

"I got it from a little shop that sells old stuff. It's from the 1950s, and since, well, you don't see your friend from then, you at least have me."

"Yeah, I get it," said Peggy with a shy smile. "That's uhhh, sweet?"

"Yeah, sweet's a good word. Please stop me from eating these," he said, rubbing his hands together as a gesture of fait accompli.

"Sorry, I didn't get you anything," said Peggy.

"Oh, that's okay. I like surprising people. Okay, don't be a stranger. I'm going now." Fran got up and extended his arms, expecting a hug.

"How's Larry?" she said, hugging him back in a cordial embrace.

"Mean as ever. But he now has a dog-sitting business because he prefers animals to people."

"A dog-sitting service?"

"Sure, it's a booming business these days. People have dogs like kids. I saw him the other day with three Rottweilers on leashes. You'd need his muscles to handle that crew."

Peggy laughed out loud, picturing Larry in a *Hounds of Baskerville* scenario, barking louder than any of the canines in his company. "Tell him I said hello, if you see him," she said, wiping confectioner's sugar on her black sweater sleeve.

"Yeah, he says he'll never talk to me again and then calls me two days later. It's worse than a teenage romance. Larry is my cross to bear." Fran pulled on his golden brown cap and headed to the door. "Thank your mom for the cookies, and…uh, Happy New Year."

Walking down the pathway, she noticed he had a slight limp as if one leg was a tiny bit shorter than the other, or some other physical malady. Possibly a knee injury or, God forbid, more growing pains since he was already hovering at six foot five. *Would he stay in my life*, she wondered as he disappeared, the dusky afternoon light swallowing up any remaining sight of him. She placed the pretty, faded pin, its ceramic petals bright and cheery against the drab cotton weave.

All of these images flooded her head as she pushed a few more squishy snowmen with carrot noses and stovepipe hats into their new home next to prayerful angels with golden curls and pearly white wings.

Reaching down into a box of broken items, she pulled out a silver and gold glittery sign with a single satin red ribbon, missing a similar strand from the other end, intended to hold it in place for hanging on a wall or door. The engraved words in elegant script were: "*Que suenes con los angeles.*"

She yelled over to her new coworker, "Hey, Lily, what does this mean?"

Lily wiped her hands on her apron and studied the sign. "Aah, it says, 'May you dream of angels.'"

Peggy gave the slightest grin before breaking out into a canyon-sized smile. "I did better than that. I met one."

Epilogue

Year 2075. Miriam packed her grandchildren—all three of them—into her dome-shaped car, charged and ready for a fifty-mile drive.

"Okay, sweethearts. Are we ready for an old-fashioned road trip?"

The twin girls, Margaret and Mary, age ten, and Michael, age seven, raced into the small car as an energetic and fresh-faced Miriam, age sixty-five, lifted the bubble-shaped door and window ensemble. Piled in the back, their expectations grew.

"Where are we going again, Gran?" piped Michael, jumping up and down as he sat in between nature's bookends, Margaret and Mary.

"It's a surprise," she said. Gleaming windmills towered along the pristine highway, spinning and waving their appendages and powering white bungalows with white roofs dotting the scenery like lambs grazing on hillsides. *So much white*, she thought. Whatever happened to color?

Energy conservation had changed her life, everyone's life. White was green, a word and concept that had lasted for decades now, like a rock 'n' roll band still playing fifty years later. Gas stations were a rarity as were gas-fueled vehicles, an icon of past glory days. Her bubble of a vehicle, now twenty years old, was nearly obsolete, replaced by solar-powered everything that moved without sheer human locomotion. Thirty minutes later, on a steamy, humid July morning, the foursome approached the metropolis of Washington DC. The petite Miriam, barely five foot two, with a face like a porcelain doll framing light gray eyes, looked more like an adventuresome babysitter than a grandmother. Her shoulder-length hair was touched up by a roll-on dye adding attractive highlighted streaks of shimmering red-gold that complemented her gold T-shirt and purposely faded skirt with its ten vibrant shades ranging from crimson to a peachy orange. Anything to offset a white and green world. Even black attracted her because it contained every color of the spectrum, hidden, blended, and masked. She certainly hoped and prayed heaven would have brilliant gold and gemstones of ruby red, emerald, topaz, and sapphire blue.

The sun-drenched monuments were nearing their third century of prominence signifying and symbolizing the nation's capital, but nowhere near the antiquity of Rome's Coliseum, Athens's Parthenon, or even London's Tower (of terror) somehow preserved from going the way of the Seven Ancient Wonders of the World. Parking in a vast underground lot, they emerged on avenues and boulevards like a pioneering team of explorers. So few people took road trips, tied to a virtual life inside the comfort of their domiciles.

"We could've visited this place from my room," said a tired, whiney Michael, unaccustomed to walking long city blocks, especially on hot, paved sidewalks and streets.

"We're not doing the virtual thing, Michael sweetie. I want to show you something, up close and real."

They entered the Smithsonian with its hallmark exhibits of everything American, almost everything. In a special wing devoted to ornithology, Miriam led her small pack past various birds—all sizes—peering with fine, brilliant, or glossy feathers and glass eyes, some in midflight, others protecting a nest, or perched upon artificial tree limbs. At the end of the aisle stood one lone feather: a long, white streak with the barest touch of blush pink, unlike anything of a typical avian nature.

"About sixty years ago, I found the feather you see behind the glass."

"No way," said Margaret, with disbelief that her grandma would have any contribution to the most important museum in the world, or at least in her own country.

"It's true, I was younger than Michael here," said Miriam, folding her arms in her best retired professor pose. Her study of ornithology had led to innumerable lectures, a handful of books, and thousands of students over her tenure at Rice University in Houston, Texas, and as guest professor at Ornithology Research Centers throughout the world.

"Why is it behind the glass?" said the gentler Mary, with her whisperlike voice and quizzical expressions.

She's so much like her great-grandmother, thought Miriam, *such a pleasant, sweet little girl.* She thought about how she, in her own precocious youth, tested her mother endlessly with her headstrong, nonsensical ways and silently begged forgiveness, once again, from a woman who passed away nearly three decades ago. "Because, Mary, my dear. There is no other feather like it in the world. Nothing, nowhere."

"Why didn't you keep it for yourself?" said Margaret, eyeing it like a precious stone or some oddity that would entice a heist effort.

"Because, my dear Margaret, gifts are meant to be shared. Real gifts."

"But this isn't a gift, it's just a stupid feather," said a disenchanted Michael whose tender feet were hurting from the hot, pointless walk to an institutional building with its sterile environment and an artifact he preferred to visit in a virtual way.

"No, I get it, Gran," said Mary with delight-filled enthusiasm. "Someone or something meant for you to have it, so it is a gift, and then you sort of gave it to the world. I'd like to hear the story."

"Yes, Mary, dear. I think it's time you hear my story, at least what I remember."

At a nearby bench, she gathered a recalcitrant Michael to her lap and pulled out a small statue of a boy wearing royal robes, a crown adorning his head, an orb in one hand, the other with two fingers held up—a blessing and sign of peace. Mary and Margaret, eyes wide open, perched next to her, living birds amongst the dead.

Reading Group Questions and Topics for Discussion

1. Lori waits for "the right time" to make peace with her mother and confess to her misdeeds. Are there times when you have waited to make peace with a family member or friend? How did you feel during the waiting period?
2. What's the difference between a reluctant heart and a hardened heart when it comes to doing God's will?
3. Fran, the thinker, has a sudden and quick conversion. Do you think it's possible to have an overnight conversion if you're not living a faith life? Why or why not?
4. What, if any, incident do you think brought Peggy into Father O'Malley's confessional box?
5. Are there changes you've considered making in your life to draw closer to the Lord? If so, what are they?
6. Throughout salvation history, angels represent God's desire to communicate with us. Can you retell any time in your life that you felt God was speaking to you through another person?
7. When we first meet Peggy, Fran, and Larry, they are leading lives of deception with lying, cheating, and stealing. What do you think can lead a person to a destructive path, and how can it be reversed?

8. Trying harder doesn't always work when surrendering to God's will. What does work, and how can we stop from repeating the same failings?

Infant of Prague

St. Andrew's Prayer

Hail and blessed be the hour and moment

in which the Son of God

was born of the most pure Virgin Mary,

at midnight, in Bethlehem,

in piercing cold.

In that hour,

vouchsafe, O my God!

to hear my prayer and grant my desires,

through the merits of Our Saviour Jesus Christ,

and of His Blessed Mother.

Amen.